# MISTLETOE DETOUR

THE SCOTTISH BILLIONAIRES

M. S. PARKER

BELMONTE PUBLISHING, LLC

This book is a work of fiction. The names, characters, places and incidents are products of the writer's imagination or have been used fictitiously and are not to be construed as real. Any resemblance to persons, living or dead, actual events, locales or organizations is entirely coincidental. V1

Copyright © 2023 Belmonte Publishing LLC

Published by Belmonte Publishing LLC

# THE SCOTTISH BILLIONAIRES READING ORDER

*Alec & Lumen:*
Prequel
1. Off Limits
2. Breaking Rules
3. Mending Fate

*Eoin & Aline:*
1. Strangers in Love
2. Dangers of Love

*Brody & Freedom:*
1. Single Malt
2. Perfect Blend

*Baylen & Harlee:*
Business or Pleasure

THE SCOTTISH BILLIONAIRES READING ORDER

*Drake & Maggie:*
At First Sight

*Carson & Vix:*
*A Dress for Curves*

*Spencer & London*
*A Play for Love*

## BOOK DESCRIPTION

"Mistletoe Detour," the latest entry in the Scottish Billionaire series by M. S. Parker, sends readers off on a hilarious, heartwarming holiday road trip.

Blaze Gracen, a renowned Johns Hopkins professor, gears up for a festive family shindig in sunny San Ramon. However, Mother Nature has other ideas, and a surprise winter storm leaves his flight stranded in not-so-tropical Chicago.

Enter Trisha Easton, a quick-witted New Yorker with a suitcase full of sass and a knack for turning lemons into spiked lemonade. Also stranded in Chicago, she opts for a daring, map-defying drive across the country to San Francisco – because who needs a flight when you've got audacity and a playlist of classic road trip tunes?

Their paths cross at a car rental counter more crowded than a Black Friday sale, leading to a spontaneous decision to travel together. Vowing to keep their pasts as hidden as their luggage in the trunk, they embark on a road trip filled with gut-busting banter and an undeniable sizzle that would thaw even the frostiest winter road.

But as they zigzag through snowy landscapes and quaint towns, Blaze and Trisha's laid-back "let's just be road trip buddies" agreement faces more challenges than a high school final.

This latest installment in the Scottish Billionaire series isn't just a story of unexpected romance but a holiday escapade with the possibility of lasting love. Will their journey end with a simple 'thank you for the memories,' or will the mistletoe work its festive magic?

Buckle up for "Mistletoe Detour," where love, laughter, and a sprinkle of holiday magic are just around the next snow-covered bend.

ONE

*BLAZE*

I must have been a masochist in my previous life. That's the only logical explanation for my decision to fly from Baltimore to San Ramon for the holidays. Initially, I had planned to leave the day before Christmas Eve, a prospect possibly even more chaotic. However, a problem with my building's heating system forced me into a hotel two days ago, prompting me to take an earlier flight. It seemed more practical to head home sooner rather than to linger in a hotel room for days.

As I made my way down the aisle looking for my seat, a sudden shove against my back caused me to stumble forward. Grasping the seat back in front of me, I steadied myself, receiving a disapproving glance from the dark-haired man seated there. Looking over my shoulder, I restrained a sharp comment when I saw an older woman struggling with her bag. She tugged at it again, narrowly missing my hip with her elbow.

"Can I help you with that?" I offered, ignoring the impatient stares from the line behind us.

"Thank you, young man," she gratefully responded, her smile widening as I hoisted the cumbersome bag into the overhead compartment she pointed out.

As I eased into my seat, I stretched my legs with a deep exhale. At six feet one inch, I wasn't the tallest in my family - that honor belonged to my younger brother Fury - but my height made me fully appreciate the perks of first-class travel, especially on a lengthy journey like this.

I waited until the flight attendants finished their routine announcements before pulling out my phone to check my emails. Even though I was on vacation for the next week, I liked to stay updated on work. Last week, Johns Hopkins University's semester ended, and thanks to no final papers, I could prepare for next semester's classes. Although I was ahead of schedule, I had no intention of slacking off.

After I checked my email, I set my phone aside, thinking how excited I was to see my family, especially my younger brother, Fury, and our little sister, Rose.

With me living in Baltimore, Fury in California, and Rose in Colorado, our opportunities to meet were scarce. However, we kept in touch through frequent phone calls and messages.

I sometimes wondered whether my parents would have approved my decision to pursue a doctorate far away. I would never know. They passed away when I was eleven, and my aunt Theresa Carideo and her husband Patrick McCrae took us all in. We had a great upbringing, but being the oldest, I always felt responsible for my siblings. It was hard to leave them for college, and the years in between hadn't made it any easier.

Despite that, they were fine without me. The business Fury had started with our step-cousin/brother, Cory, was thriving, and Rose, with her veterinary degree from Colorado State University, had recently purchased a horse ranch.

Hence, the reason I was traveling during the holidays. It wasn't because I was a masochist in a previous life. This Holiday would be a rare event: we would all be together.

A chime signaled an announcement from the cockpit. "This is your captain speaking. We'll be beginning our descent into Chicago shortly. Please be aware that we may encounter some rough weather, so expect a bit of turbulence. For your safety, stay seated with your seatbelts fastened."

The seatbelt light illuminated, and a buzz of concern spread through the cabin. Flight attendants moved along the aisles, offering reassurances. While they weren't thrilled with the captain's mention of weather challenges, their professionalism continued as they prepared us for landing.

A perky blonde stewardess sauntered past me as I sat in my window seat, contemplating how much I hated flying. She gave me a flirty wink and gently brushed her hand against my shoulder, enough to let me know she might be interested in more than just serving drinks during our upcoming stopover. I might have been tempted if I hadn't been in a hurry.

Since my disastrous marriage ended twelve years ago, I've stuck with casual relationships and fleeting connections. Occasionally, someone would try to take it to the next level, resulting in our breakup.

The flight attendant seemed like a low-risk dalliance, but I wouldn't risk missing my connecting flight for a brief fling.

But I could be tempted if we crossed paths again on my return flight.

The plane touched down safely, and I disembarked, swiftly heading to my next gate, relying on my knowledge of the airport. But my speedy pace came to a stop when I spotted a crowd of people glued to a flight information screen. Looking up, I saw all flights were marked "DELAYED."

"Fuck," I muttered under my breath.

Being familiar with this airport, I immediately headed for the nearest lounge. Glaring at the flight status screens for the next hour wouldn't alter my circumstances, but maybe a drink could ease the growing anxiety.

The lounge was rapidly reaching capacity, yet I found a vacant seat at the bar. "A whisky, neat," I said as the bartender drew near. "Your finest selection."

Although I wasn't a McCrae by blood, growing up within their family circle had cultivated my taste for Scotch and whisky. Brody, the eldest on the McCrae side, had a penchant for crafting his own whisky brands and generously sharing them, thus spoiling us all.

The first sip from my glass confirmed that this whisky was comparable to Brody's recent concoction.

"Layover or delay?" The gray-haired man beside me inquired, turning slightly toward me.

"Delayed on a layover," I replied. "What about you?"

"Same," he sighed, draining his glass. "But with the weather being what it is, I doubt we're leaving anytime soon."

I noticed a slight slur in his speech, making me wonder how long he'd been drinking here. But worry about the weather overshadowed my curiosity. Being stuck in this airport with a crowd of Christmas travelers was my worst nightmare.

I took a cautious sip of my whiskey, refraining from the temptation to quickly finish it and order another. Keeping alert seemed wise, particularly considering the mayhem that would ensue if multiple flights were grounded. The airport would become chaotic as people frantically searched for alternative travel options. However, I would go all out if they officially canceled my flight—anything to dull the surrounding nightmare.

A hockey game was being shown on the bar's TV when the man next to me started talking again. He was excited about the game, and under different circumstances, I might have found his commentary entertaining. Now, he was just annoying.

I finished my drink as an announcement echoed through the lounge, confirming my worst fear: icy conditions had grounded all outgoing flights. The airlines would handle accommodations, refunds, and ticket exchanges.

An appeal for cooperation concluded the announcement, barely audible over the clamor of frustrated passengers.

Merry fucking Christmas.

# TWO

## *TRISHA*

I HAD ALWAYS PROMISED MYSELF THAT SOMEDAY I would buy first-class tickets, and as our plane descended into Chicago, I wished that day was today.

Between the lascivious older man in the seat across the aisle who couldn't tear his eyes from my chest all flight long, the sniffling toddler behind me who repeatedly kicked my seat, and the anxious woman with flight anxiety to my right who kept clutching my arm every time the plane was jostled in the slightest, I was beginning to believe it would've been preferable to drive from New York City to San Francisco. I simply prayed none of these people would follow me onto my connecting flight.

The way my life had been going for the last few months, however, I doubted I'd be that lucky.

"We're gonna crash. We're gonna crash." The woman beside me started chanting as the seat belt light came on.

"We're not going to crash," I reassured her with the same sympathetic smile that had become my default since we boarded, though it was beginning to wane. I sympathized with her fear, but lacked the energy to continue comforting her while dealing with my own concerns.

Like the reason for my trip back to California for Christmas, even though I had just been there for Thanksgiving.

I hoped my dad wouldn't get into a fit when I proposed the idea of him moving to Baltimore with me. He had been living with diabetes since I turned sixteen, but his recent diagnosis of glomerulonephritis had made the situation more serious. He insisted he had faith in his regular doctor. However, he ended up in the hospital before his kidney problem was discovered. Therefore, I didn't fully trust the elderly Dr. Dyson to take care of my father's health.

I tried to convince my dad to move to New York with me, but the cost of living there meant I couldn't afford a bigger apartment. I doubted my father could find a job given his recent health problems, even though he wasn't yet fifty and worked hard. Also, getting health insurance would be difficult.

So I could understand why he objected.

That was all in the past. I hadn't told my dad yet, but months ago, I applied for a job in Baltimore, and now I'd gotten hired at Johns Hopkins. This move would allow me to get my dad to the best kidney doctor in the country, and I would not take no for an answer.

I reminded myself that I could do this. I'd earned a doctorate in education and a master's in technology management from Columbia at twenty-three. Teaching high school students at one of NYC's worst schools had been a choice, not a necessity.

The woman beside me now squeezed my arm to the point where I was sure I'd have bruises, but the severe turbulence as we descended into Chicago made me sympathetic to her fear, so I didn't say anything.

As we landed safely, she finally let go of my aching arm.

My layover was for an hour, so I didn't rush off the plane. Instead, I took my time heading for my gate, enjoying the thrum of excitement from all the Christmas travelers and the wide-eyed looks on the faces of kids who hadn't been in an airport before.

One of my favorite things about traveling during the holidays was people-watching.

After finding my gate, I took a sip from my water

bottle, sat, and leaned back, stretching my legs. Soon enough, I overheard people discussing the worsening weather, mentioning the intensifying wind from the lake and the decreasing temperature.

Having lived in New York City for almost half my life, I wasn't worried. Instead, I smiled at the thought of the warmer, sunnier climate waiting for me on the West Coast.

Suddenly, I heard a commotion. As I was heading in that direction to see what was happening, an announcement said that they had canceled all outgoing flights. Passengers groaned and sighed with defeat throughout the terminal, their shoulders slumping.

My eyes darted from the departure board to the ticketing counter to the windows, revealing a blizzard battering the tarmac outside.

Each possibility flickered through my mind - staying overnight at a hotel while praying for a change in the weather, booking a bus ticket, calling a friend. Yeah, right. The mounting snowdrifts and howling wind could soon eliminate each option one by one.

I bit my lip, gears churning to chart an alternative course to my final destination. The storm may have diverted my original route, but I wouldn't let it deter my journey altogether. There had to be a way.

As the blizzard raged outside, I had an absurd, yet irresistible, idea.

Swiveling on my feet, I made a beeline for the long-distance rental car counter, silently grateful for the small carry-on that spared me the hassle of retrieving checked baggage. Even so, a queue had formed at the rental desk, snaking its way through the terminal.

With a sigh, I stood behind a dark-haired woman with two teenagers and pulled out my phone. Since Dad had planned to pick me up when I landed in California and knew he'd want to know about my change in plans anyway, I sent a long message explaining everything. By the time I pocketed my phone, the trio in front of me had finished their paperwork, and I stepped up to the counter.

"I'd like to rent a car." I gave the harried-looking woman behind the desk my best smile, knowing she was probably getting an earful from the other stranded passengers.

"For how long?" she asked.

"As long as it takes to drive to San Francisco."

If my answer surprised her, she didn't show it. She just entered the information into the computer and moved on to the next question. I tried not to wince at the woman's estimate but reminded myself that I'd bought the ticket insurance, which meant the final cost wouldn't be too bad. Still, I would have to use some of my signing bonus from Johns Hopkins to cover it. Even that didn't deter me, though. I'd latched on to the idea of driving across the country, and now I would not let anything stop me.

She handed me the paperwork, and I stepped aside to organize my belongings before proceeding to the pickup point. However, an irate voice sliced through the cacophony before I could make much progress.

"What do you mean there aren't any cars left?"

The clamor of the rental lobby ebbed for a moment, and my gaze lifted to catch the spectacle unfolding next to me. A man stood with narrowed eyes and a frown etched onto his face.

"I'm sorry, sir, but I just rented out the last one." She set a sign down on the table. "I was just getting ready to put this out."

The acrylic sign caught the light, casting a shadow that deepened the scowl on the man's face, stormy eyes intensifying. His lips curved around the words that followed, each one laced with the simmering impatience that desk clerks everywhere know all too well—the kind that brokers no simple answers or quick fixes.

"Do you know who I am?" When the woman didn't answer, he spun around, dark eyes blazing with anger as he searched the crowd. I didn't realize who he was looking for until he spotted me and took a few steps toward me. "You took my car."

"Apologies for snagging the last one, but you're not

alone in needing to get places," I remarked, showing the queue behind him.

"I don't give a fuck about them," he snapped as he took another few steps toward me. "You're going to give me that car, understand?"

I straightened my posture and steeled my nerves. Should he dare touch me, he'd quickly discover why I'd never been afraid of living in New York City.

Before he reached me, however, a tall body moved between us. My eyes traveled up from thick thighs straining a pair of jeans to a very nice ass, a broad back, broader shoulders, then curly red hair.

"Back the fuck off, or you'll regret it."

His deep, rumbling voice made my stomach twist. Still, it clearly affected the angry man differently because I didn't hear another word from him. A moment later, my rescuer turned to reveal a ruggedly handsome face and stunning blue-violet eyes.

Well, damn. A genuine knight in shining armor.

## THREE

*BLAZE*

THE AIRPORT PLUNGED INTO UTTER CONFUSION AS people struggled with the unforeseen situation. Amid the turmoil, while trying to figure out my next step, a man's irate voice pierced the noise. Others might have hesitated, but even before my parents died, I couldn't just stand by when someone acted like a bully.

Therefore, I ended up between a woman and an angry jerk who wanted the car she'd rented.

When he retreated, still frowning, I turned to the woman but was left speechless by what I saw.

A cascade of chestnut curls fell just past her shoulders, prompting thoughts of how they'd look spread out on my pillow. My eyes swept over her figure, neither concealed by her plain clothes nor overtly displayed.

She was dressed like many of us on flights, prioritizing comfort over style. When I looked into her electric blue eyes, I saw amusement and realized she had caught me openly checking her out. Shit.

"Blaze Gracen." I held out a hand as I introduced myself. "Are you all right?"

"Trisha Easton," she said, shaking my hand with a surprisingly firm grip. "I'm good. Thanks for the assist."

"Always." I blurted, then grinned. "Beats pacing the terminal like a caged animal, being stuck here."

Her eyes twinkled as she gave me the same sort of once-over that I'd just given her, and I felt my body heat under her gaze.

"Here's a crazy idea. How about you ride shotgun to protect this hot mess from handsy truckers?" She winked. "I mean, I can throw a mean right hook if I gotta, but having a beefcake bodyguard to scare 'em off first would be nice. And you're also easy on the eyes, so..."

I asked where she was headed, swearing it wasn't just her flirting, making me curious.

"San Francisco," she said, sauntering toward the rental counter.

I followed, already shaking my head at her reckless plan. "You're seriously road-tripping from Chicago to San Francisco solo?"

"What, you think I can't hack it 'cause I'm a

chick?" She was playing, but I heard the edge in her voice.

"Hey, any woman who wants to drive cross-country has every right to, you do you." I meant it. "But if my sisters made that trek alone, especially in winter, I'd worry."

She stopped and gave me a searching look that seemed to see right into the very heart of me.

"Where are you on your way to?"

"Family in San Ramon," I said. "It's near–"

"I know what it's near." She smiled at me. "I grew up in the area."

"Makes sense why we're both stuck here," I said. Then I looked at the rental agreement in her hand. "Well, I'm stuck. You've got a way out."

"You know," she said slowly, "I was maybe joking before, but how about I make that offer real?"

"What offer?"

"To ride with me," she said. "It's a long drive to make alone. I'll have to stop to sleep, stretch my legs, keep awake. But the trip could be done in half the time if I had someone take turns driving."

My eyebrows shot up. "Are you seriously asking a stranger to drive across the country with you? I'm pretty sure that's how horror movies start."

"Or Hallmark movies."

Her widening grin triggered a surge of desire that

left me paralyzed for a moment. Not even during my marriage with Ava had I felt such an intense, primal response.

"You really trust me that much? A complete stranger?" I asked skeptically.

She shrugged. "I've got this sixth sense about people." Then she held up her phone and snapped a pic. "But just in case you turn out to be a serial killer, I'm sending your mug to my dad. That way, if I vanish somewhere along the Mississippi, he'll know who to hunt down."

"Why wait for the Mississippi?" I deadpanned. "I could get rid of you back in St. Louis."

She cackled as she handed her ticket to the attendant.

"We need some rules," she said, glancing at me. "Not for safety or driving, but so we don't actually end up in a Hallmark movie."

"Not a fan?" I asked.

"I've occasionally indulged," she said. "But I don't want to star in a real live one. Do you?"

I laughed and shook my head. "No, I'm not that much of a romantic."

"Good."

She didn't hide the attraction in her eyes, and I knew my own heated the same way when I looked at her. Physically wanting her differed from romantically wanting her, at least for me, but I didn't dare to ask if she felt the same. Since we would be in a car together for two days, I didn't want to jeopardize our easy banter.

"Rule number one: dodge every cheesy cliché like the plague," she declared. "That means zero bedroom mix-ups like sharing a double-bed and avoiding quaint snow-globe towns with twinkle lights."

"And absolutely no mistletoe meet-cutes," I chimed in.

"Spot on." Her laughter was infectious. "But for real, let's keep it to the fun shit; no dating interviews. I don't want to know what you do for a living, and I don't even wanna know which city you flew in from. This is *not* a date. Agree?"

My head nodded in agreement as she continued. "We can shoot the breeze about our dysfunctional family holidays or debate if *Die Hard* is a Christmas flick. Just promise me there's not a pissed-off significant other who's gonna hunt me down for hijacking her dude."

"First off, *Die Hard* is a Christmas movie—end of story. And second? There's no ball and chain here." I eyed her left hand, casually perched on her luggage. "Your turn. Will I find an angry boyfriend in my DMs, or are you flying solo?"

Given that she mentioned sending my photo and

name to her father, not her boyfriend, I doubted it, but I still wanted to be certain. My rationale was that I didn't want to be in a situation where a guy would punch me in the face for hitching a ride with his girlfriend. Then another part of me wanted to know if she was taken; if being attracted to her was okay.

"No," she said, her eyes softening. "I'm also single."

The intercom called her name before I could say anything else. The car was ready.

"Coming?"

It might have been one of the dumbest things I'd ever done, but I would do it anyway. And deep down, I felt that this decision could change everything.

"Lead the way."

She did. And I followed.

## FOUR

### *TRISHA*

THIS WAS EITHER GOING TO BE THE BEST IDEA I'D ever had or the worst. I didn't really see a whole lot of room for anything in between.

When Blaze didn't object to me driving, I knew he wasn't some arrogant jerk going all alpha on me at some point, even though he'd gallantly rescued me at the airport.

Some say intuition is nonsense, but my dad taught me to trust my gut, especially with guys. Coupled with my experience moving alone cross-country for college at sixteen, I felt pretty good about gauging people.

We barely spoke as we drove out of the city. I needed to focus on navigating the unfamiliar, icy streets. Fortunately, the car had good snow tires. Once we reached the city limits and got onto the main highway heading west, I felt relaxed enough to ask Blaze to find us some music for our drive.

"What's your poison?" he asked.

"Take a guess," I challenged, flicking a glance his way. When he raised an eyebrow, I added, "It's not like we don't have the time."

He smirked, a slow burn as he studied me with his gorgeous eyes. I felt my body warming, making me wonder what it would be like to literally be bare under his gaze. "I'm getting a strong bubblegum pop vibe from you," he mused, "but there's a twist there, isn't there? People don't peg you right, do they?"

Heat crept up my neck, and I kept my gaze locked on the frosty road. Was I that transparent, or was he some kind of savant?

He chuckled, nailing it. "Classic rock, huh?"

"You could say I'm genre-fluid," I admitted, "but yeah, classic rock holds the crown."

He grinned as he reached for the radio. "My college roommate was a major Dead Head."

I snorted, "Total Van Halen junkie here." He sifted through the stations, giving each a brief nod before moving on. "My dad was a grease monkey and the shop always blasted VH. He'd scoop me up, windows down, screaming 'Panama' as his life depended on it."

His eyes flickered, "Tight with your old man?"

"Mom bailed at six months. Just me and Pops."

"I'm sorry—"

I cut off his pity. "Dad's a rock star in his own right. You? Family man or lone wolf?"

It seemed like the natural question to ask after his, but the moment it came out, I saw his expression tighten minutely, and I regretted my question. I tried telling him he didn't need to respond, but he'd already started talking.

"My parents passed away when I was eleven. Car accident. My aunt raised my siblings and me after that." He managed a smile, but it didn't reach his eyes.

"I'm sorry for your loss," I said sincerely, reaching over to lay a hand on his arm.

"Thank you." He put a hand over mine but didn't remove it right away, the heat from his skin warming mine. "And I'm sorry your mom left you."

"One-half mile ahead, keep left."

The car's GPS voice had me jerking back my hand as if I'd just remembered that I was driving.

"Can you check the weather on your phone?" I asked. "We should probably keep an eye on it as we go."

As the miles stretched on, the tension waned, replaced by the rhythmic hum of the highway beneath. Blaze was hotter than hell, but I held back any thoughts of suggesting a motel stop. With my whole life about to be turned upside down after Christmas, the last thing I needed was to get entangled with a guy I just met.

"So, let me get this straight," I quipped. "Your aunt hooks up with a Scotsman who's already got a freaking soccer team?"

Blaze grinned. "Alec, the twins Brody and Cory, Eoin, and little Miss Maggie."

"And your aunt threw in her own squad, right?"

"Yep, the globe-trotters: Austin, Rome, Paris, Aspen."

"Their baby-making didn't tap out there?"

"Sean and Xander - a twofer - followed by London." He laughed at my gape. "Add to that motley crew me, Fury, and Rose."

I whistled. "I pictured family game night, not a family reunion. That's a full-blown dynasty."

Blaze's smile softened. "Being one of the big dogs meant I was tripping over toddlers. But honestly? It was pretty great."

I started asking questions about the other kids, and his stories carried us over the Mississippi River, where we stopped for gas and so I could take a picture.

"Now take one with me," I demanded after I'd gotten one of me alone.

"It's freezing out here," he argued.

"Too bad." I grabbed his arm and dragged him over

to the shore. I leaned against him and smiled, then snapped a selfie of us, laughing when I saw the scowl on Blaze's face.

"Can we go now?" he asked. "I'm truly freezing my balls off."

The color in his cheeks, not entirely from the brisk wind, tempted me to tease him about it, but he was right about it being cold, so I just nodded, and we headed back, with him taking the wheel.

I must've fallen asleep at some point because we were approaching Des Moines by the time I woke up. The rhythmic pulse of the road beneath us melded with Led Zeppelin's "Ramble On" streaming through the speakers. The landscape blanketed in snow flew by in a serene blur.

"You hungry?" Blaze's voice cut through the music.

I glanced at him before peering out at the passing signs for food and gas. "Starving," I confessed. "I didn't realize how much time had passed."

He pointed to an upcoming exit. "Diner up ahead. Looks like it could be decent."

"Perfect," I said, and he flicked on the turn signal and steered us toward a hopeful food stop.

We pulled into a spot outside a quaint little place with neon lights that flickered 'Open' in a comforting, if not slightly kitschy, way. The wind nipped at my cheeks as we made our way inside, escaping the biting cold for the warm embrace of greasy spoons and vinyl booths.

As we slid into a booth by the window, Blaze's presence felt more tangible than before, like heat emanating from a fire I wasn't sure I should play with. The waitress came over with menus, her smile tired but genuine as she poured us coffee without asking if we wanted any. It was assumed—a warm-up from the chill.

"What's good here?" Blaze asked her.

She chuckled. "Honey, everything's good here. But if you're looking for something special, our meatloaf is famous around these parts."

Blaze glanced at me with an eyebrow quirked in question.

I nodded. "Let's split it? And maybe a side of fries?"

"Make it two sides," he added with a smile that made my heart do an odd little skip.

As she walked away to put in our order, Blaze turned his attention back to me. "So, Trisha Easton," he began, casually leaning back against the booth. "I know we agreed on no personal stuff, but I gotta know; what drives you crazy? What's your pet peeve?"

I laughed at the abruptness of his question, but played along. "People who don't use turn signals," I said without hesitation.

He nodded approvingly. "A woman after my own heart."

"And you? Blaze Gracen," I mirrored his tone. "What grinds your gears?"

He thought for a moment before answering, "Lack of punctuality."

I raised an eyebrow. "Time is valuable?"

"To me, it is." He gave me a look that said there was more to it than that.

The food arrived, and I forked a piece of the famous meatloaf, its steam curling up like a siren's call. "If this tastes half as good as it smells, we've hit the jackpot."

Blaze watched with an amused glint in his eye. "Prepare for your taste buds to throw a party."

The first bite was a revelation—savory, rich, and comforting. "Holy cow, this *is* good," I mumbled, mouth still full.

"Right?" Blaze savored his own bite, his approval was evident.

We fell into a peaceful rhythm of eating and light banter. It was nice, almost too nice, actually. Dangerous for my well-set boundaries.

The waitress sauntered back to our table, a twinkle in her eye that matched the garish lights strung up around the diner. She held a Santa hat in her hand, stretching it out toward Blaze with a grin that could melt the snow outside.

"Hey there, handsome," she said, her voice syrupy sweet. "Mind giving us a Christmas smile for our wall? You'd look mighty fine in this here hat."

I raised an eyebrow at Blaze, unable to suppress the smirk tugging at my lips. "Looks like someone's made an impression."

He shot me a sideways glance, a silent challenge in his blue-violet eyes. "Jealous?"

I scoffed. "Please, I'm just looking out for you. Wouldn't want you to get swept off your feet by every charming waitress from here to San Francisco."

He accepted the hat from her, his fingers brushing hers as he did so—a touch that lingered just a tad too long for mere politeness. "Only if I get to keep the hat," he declared.

The waitress giggled, a sound as fluffy as the whipped cream on top of our pie. "All yours, sugar."

With the grace of someone who'd done this before —perhaps during his college days—Blaze donned the Santa hat and posed beside our booth.

"Get in next to him, sugar," the waitress said. She pulled out a Polaroid camera from behind the counter and snapped the picture.

As she shook the developing photo in her hand,

Blaze looked at me with that Santa hat perched jauntily on his head and raised an eyebrow.

"So, what do you think? Does it bring out my eyes?"

I bit back laughter, focusing on my pie instead. "Absolutely," I deadpanned. "Santa's never looked so ruggedly handsome."

The waitress slipped away after pinning the photo on their wall of fame—a collection of strangers bound by shared moments within these walls—and Blaze pulled off the hat, tossing it between us.

"Should I be worried about competition?" I asked.

He leaned back and gave me a look that was half-mock seriousness and half-amused indulgence. "Only if you think you can't handle the heat?" he said smoothly.

"Trust me," I shot back with a laugh. "The only heat I'm worried about is from that meatloaf."

Blaze reached across the table for another fry, smirking beneath that ridiculous Santa hat still sitting between us like some holiday mascot gone rogue.

"I'll have you know," he said between bites, "I've never lost a meatloaf battle."

I glanced at him from under my lashes. "That so? Because I'm pretty sure I'm about to witness your first defeat."

He laughed, low and rich, and for a moment, everything else faded away—the snow outside, the miles we still had to go, even my well-guarded heart that wasn't supposed to get involved.

A burly man at the counter grumbled into his phone loud enough for the entire diner to hear. "Yeah, storm's barreling in faster than expected."

I shot Blaze a look. "We should probably get moving if we're going to stay ahead of it."

He nodded, wiping his mouth with a napkin. "Agreed."

We hustled to pay, and with one last look at our picture on the wall—a testament to our shared journey—I followed him out into the snowy night.

Back on the road, the car's heater blasted against the creeping chill as we pushed forward into the vast expanse of America's heartland.

"So," I ventured, tapping my fingers against my knee, "what's the strategy for outrunning a storm?"

Blaze glanced at me with mock seriousness. "Speed and cunning," he said. "And your impeccable choice in travel companions."

I laughed, rolling my eyes. "Modesty clearly isn't your strong suit."

He grinned that half-cocked smile that did funny things to my insides. "I left that back at the diner with half our fries."

We sped through Iowa and into Nebraska, pausing

just for gas and to switch drivers so Blaze could catch some sleep, having not slept yet. Whether we were chatting, singing to the radio, or sitting quietly, the spark between us lingered—an electric jolt when our eyes locked, a longing in my fingers to reach for him.

Once he dozed off, I could freely steal looks without the fear of him catching me ogling him.

I hadn't planned on disturbing him, but as we neared the place where Route 80 passed near the Colorado border, traffic slowed to a crawl. Blaze jolted awake as I hit the brakes for the umpteenth time. "What's the holdup?" he mumbled, rubbing his eyes like he could scrub away the gridlock.

"Some kind of snafu up ahead. No clue why; we're in the middle of nowhere."

"Let's see if the radio's got the scoop." He turned the dial just in time for the bad news.

"Christ, a sixteen-car circus act," Blaze groaned, killing the radio. "Did we miss the 76 exit yet?"

"Nah, it's up the road. We could reroute through 76 to 70," I suggested, "though it'll tack on a good three hours."

He let out a grumble. "Fantastic. I guess that beats rotting here."

"Yes, I'd rather not risk being stuck if we need gas or a bathroom." I grinned at him. "Not all of us can just use an empty bottle."

Blaze rolled his eyes and ignored my jab, his fingers dancing over the GPS, desperate for a magic path through the chaos.

"I've heard Colorado is just as stunning as Wyoming," I remarked. "It would be cool to visit the Mile-High City. Once, I had a layover in Denver, but all I saw was the airport interior."

He sounded annoyed as he replied, "This was simply the quickest way. I told my aunt when I'd get to the house based on that."

"They'll understand," I reassured him. "Let's take 76, stop at the first rest area, and update everyone. We don't want them worrying, and we'll still make it back before Christmas Eve."

"Yeah," he agreed, sinking into his seat with a sigh. "I just hate when plans get disrupted."

"I notice that," I said with a smile at his irritation. "But maybe there's a different way to view this."

"Like how?" he inquired, his voice tinged with curiosity.

"Think of it not as an inconvenience but an adventure," I suggested, stealing a glance his way and feeling that familiar warmth in my stomach. "Like the canceled flights. If it weren't for that, we wouldn't have met, and I'm really enjoying our journey together."

For what felt like a long minute, his gaze rested on me, and I fought the urge to fidget.

"Fine," he finally conceded, not concealing his hesitance. "I'll try to see this as another adventure."

"Good."

"Still, I'm crossing my fingers for no more surprises."

# FIVE

## *BLAZE*

I KNEW WISHING FOR NO MORE SURPRISES COULD be a bad omen, and I fully blamed myself when thick white flakes began falling on the road ahead. Despite traffic from the detour, we had made good time to Denver, with the weather staying gray and cold until we reached the city limits. That's when flurries started, remaining periodic until we passed through Denver. Then the snow steadily intensified.

With the city at least an hour behind us now, the conditions had worsened enough to make me anxious as a passenger. I tried concealing my nerves, but Trisha was extremely perceptive.

"Are you okay?"

The friendly vibes we'd had from the start led me to tell her the honest truth.

"My parents died in a car crash." Saying those words still twisted my heart, though the sharp pain had faded over time.

"Oh shit, fuck. I'm so sorry, Blaze." Trisha took a hand off the wheel to reach for me, but stopped. She correctly sensed I needed to see her hands on the wheel more than a touch.

"I'm usually fine in cars," I went on. "Since I wasn't with them when it happened, most days I don't think about it. But bad weather can make me anxious sometimes."

"Like now," she said.

"Exactly."

"Would driving help you feel better?"

I looked through the windshield. My heart pounded as the visibility worsened.

"Let's stop here," Trisha said. "I know it'll add time to our trip, but—"

"Better safe than sorry," I cut in. "Is there anywhere for us to stop?"

"I saw a sign for some lodging at the next exit."

As Trisha exited the highway, we slowed to a crawl and headed for the soft pink glow the GPS said was a motel.

We found a parking spot, and even though the

snow was so thick, we couldn't see if there were lines. We grabbed our bags and headed inside, glancing at the TV as we walked to the desk. Unsurprisingly, a winter storm advisory was displayed, with details scrolling across the bottom.

I was relieved to see that the snow was supposed to stop soon after midnight and that road crews would have the roads cleared before morning, but we would definitely have to stay the night.

The desk clerk, a disinterested twenty-something, announced we had no rooms before Trisha or I could even speak.

"Not a single one?" Trisha's shoulders sagged.

"Sorry." Her tone lacked sincerity.

"Are you absolutely sure?" I pleaded.

She looked up. "There's one, but the TV's broken, and only the bathroom light works."

"We don't mind," Trisha insisted. "We just need somewhere to stay until the storm passes."

"I could get in trouble," the clerk hesitated, "especially if you stumbled in the dark..."

"How much?" I interjected, noticing a hint of opportunism in her eyes. "Twice the room rate?"

"This isn't the Hilton," she retorted. "Eighty dollars isn't enough for me to risk it."

Biting back a sigh, I took out my wallet and laid out

three hundred-dollar bills on the counter. "Will this work?"

"Blaze," Trisha tugged at my arm. "That's three hundred dollars! I can't let you cover all that."

Trisha wasn't aware of a significant fact about the McCrae-Carideo-Gracen family: we were all exceedingly wealthy.

"You paid for the rental," I pointed out as I slid the money to the clerk.

"And you've paid for gas," she countered. "And considering the cost of gas these days, you'll probably end up paying more than I did."

"Trust me, Trisha," I said with a smile. "I can afford it."

She narrowed her eyes and folded her arms, giving me a look that said she was still going to argue.

Unable to stop myself, I tapped the tip of her nose. "I'm doing this."

She sighed and glanced at the doors, clearly dreading getting back on the road more than letting me pay off the clerk for the room.

Seconds later, the clerk handed me two keycards.

"Room 214." She pointed to the other side of the lobby. "Elevators are over there. Take a right on the second floor. Checkout is at ten, and we have a complimentary breakfast from seven to nine."

"Thanks." I handed Trisha her key, and we headed for the elevators.

As we entered our room, I was relieved to find it tidy despite its modest size and slightly worn appearance.

"Were you expecting it to be dirty?" Trisha tossed her bag onto the dresser. "I sure was."

I almost agreed with her, but then I realized we had forgotten to ask about one crucial detail during our room negotiations.

The number of beds.

"Well, that figures." I motioned toward the single double bed when Trisha looked at me. "Looks like we've stumbled into a Hallmark movie scenario, after all."

Trisha chuckled. "Is this where we fight over who gets the couch?"

"I would take it," I replied, "except there's no couch, just that chair."

And sleeping in that chair was out of the question for both of us.

"It's fine. We can share the bed," Trisha offered. "But I call first dibs on the shower."

"Go ahead," I replied. "I'll text Theresa to let her know we're running late."

While I waited, I distracted myself by searching for faster routes for San Ramon to make up for lost time.

But when Trisha emerged from the steam-filled bathroom, my focus on travel evaporated. Her eyes sparkled, her cheeks rosy with warmth.

"Don't mock my reindeer." She pointed her finger at me.

I only noticed then that she wore long-sleeved flannel pajamas adorned with reindeer wearing Santa hats. I laughed and raised my hands. "I wouldn't dare."

"Your turn," she said. "Got a favorite side of the bed?"

"The right," I answered without thinking. "Unless it's your side."

She shrugged. "I don't really have a side. I'm good wherever."

Her words brought up an image of me lying on my side of the bed as she sprawled on top of me, wearing considerably less than those pajamas.

I quickly locked myself in the bathroom and began reciting lesson plans as I showered. I only had a pair of sweats to sleep in, and if I went out there even half-hard like I was, she'd notice. I was arrogant, but I knew I was well-endowed enough that even a partial erection was going to be ... awkward.

The moment I opened the door, all that work clearing my head went to hell because the sight of her sitting in bed, her mass of curls in a messy braid, had my cock twitching. Holding the towel in front of me, I closed the bathroom door halfway so we could have some light, but not so much that we wouldn't be able to sleep.

And the dim light would, hopefully, hide my arousal.

Sleeping was going to be a bitch.

"I think your aunt replied." Trisha pointed at my phone, her eyes widening slightly as she looked at my torso.

Right. I didn't have a shirt on.

"I didn't read it," she added quickly, her face turning red. "But I saw her name."

"Thanks." I sat on the edge of the bed as I read my aunt's reply. As expected, she told me she'd rather I arrive late and in one piece than put myself in danger.

"Is everything all right?"

I glanced at Trisha as I set my phone down and slid under the covers, careful to keep some distance between us, which wasn't easy considering I was a fairly big guy and this bed was only a double, not king or queen-sized.

"Yeah, it's all right. Why?" I folded my hands behind my head to remove the temptation to have my fingers wander over to her side, just to see what would happen.

"You look annoyed. I didn't do anything, did I?"

I looked to see Trisha stretching out on her side, her head propped up on her hand.

"It's not you," I reassured her. "I just like things to go as planned. Switching to a road trip instead of another flight isn't typical for me—I'm not an impulsive guy."

"I see the value in a solid plan," she nodded. "But you have to roll with the punches sometimes. Adapting can lead to great experiences and new people in your life."

She had a point, and part of me agreed. If everything had gone as planned, I'd be in San Ramon, but I wouldn't have met Trisha. Still, no matter how much I valued meeting her, I couldn't shake the desire to manage the surrounding chaos.

And she deserved to know why I might get snippy if our trip kept hitting roadblocks.

"I get what you're saying," I said, forcing myself to meet her eyes as I spoke. "But in my life, even the good parts of an unexpected change come with pain."

Her expression softened. "Your parents?"

I nodded, my throat suddenly tight. "Losing my parents wasn't just about losing them. We had to move out of our house, leave our neighborhood, our friends, everything we'd known." My chest ached with the memories that wanted to surface.

"I put my aunt and Patrick through a lot. And they

never held it against me. I miss my parents, but I do love my family. I know how lucky I am to have them."

"But you still hate it when things get out of your control." Her voice was gentle. "Still see change as something negative."

I could feel the hint of sadness in my smile. "I guess I haven't had enough good memories associated with unexpected change to push aside the bad ones."

I had a moment to register a heated glimmer of mischief in Trisha's eyes, and then she was leaning over and pressing her lips to mine. I froze for a split second before cupping the back of her head, holding her in place as I took control of the kiss. With a moan, her mouth opened, her teeth scraping along my bottom lip. I groaned, sliding my tongue against hers.

Just as I prepared to roll her underneath me, she surprised me by moving first. With her knees on either side of my waist, she pressed her core against me, and my hips jerked. I grabbed her hips, grinding up against her so she could feel me hardening under her. She smiled against my mouth and ran her hands up my stomach, my muscles jumping and twitching under her palms. When she flexed her fingers, the pinch of her nails jolting me, I cursed, reaching up with one hand to grasp her braid. With a tug, I pulled her head back so I could look at her.

Her pupils were blown wide, leaving only the

thinnest ring of that electric blue visible. Her lips were swollen, her face flushed. She was the most beautiful thing I'd ever seen.

"What are you doing?"

She grinned and rocked against me, the layers of cloth between us chafing us both. "Giving you something good to associate with change?"

I raised an eyebrow. "Just how good are you planning on making this memory?"

She straightened, that mischief on her face again as she unbuttoned her top, letting it hang loose for a moment so that I could see a strip of fair skin leading from her belly button up to the valley between her breasts and then to her collarbone. When my eyes met hers again, she shrugged the shirt off her shoulders and let it drop.

"Go ahead." She winked at me. "You can look. Wouldn't have taken off my shirt if I didn't want you to."

My gaze dropped, taking in the view of her hardened coral-hued nipples standing out on her chest. They seemed to be begging for my touch, my lips, my tongue. My eyes traveled downward to her flat stomach, where goosebumps rose as if they were playing a symphony.

"May I?" My voice was rough, my hands flexing on

her hip and around her braid with the effort of not moving.

"Please."

The husky tone of her voice shot a bolt of desire straight to my cock. I palmed her heavy breasts, testing their weight as I brushed my thumbs across her nipples. She moaned, tipping her head back. Her hands went to my arms as I sat up, capturing one of those plump nipples in my mouth. My cock throbbed as she rocked on me, but I ignored my need to be inside her, focusing instead all of my attention on sucking and biting until her nails dug into my flesh.

"Blaze," she whimpered.

"What is it?"

"I... need..."

"What do you need, hmm?" I took her nipple between my teeth and pulled on it until she gasped. "You need to come?"

"Mm-hm." She nodded, her eyes closed.

I dropped a hand to press my fingers against her through the soft cotton. She made a soft mewling sound that had me surging up against her, flipping us so that she was under me at last. She gasped, her eyes flying open.

I put my mouth against her ear and whispered, "No coming until I'm inside your sweet cunt."

She nodded. "Yes."

Reaching one hand between us, she cupped me through my pants and I nearly exploded right then.

Fuck.

The few moments it took to grab a condom from my wallet were a godsend, giving us both time to shed our final clothes and giving me a chance to steady myself.

But not completely, because the instant the condom was on, I settled between her legs, my fingers grazing the dark curls gathered at the apex.

"Fuck, sweetheart, you're so wet for me." I slipped a finger inside her and groaned at the tight heat.

"Trisha moaned as I slid another finger into her. Her body arched off the bed, seeking more contact with my invading digits. My cock throbbed in anticipation, straining against its confines.

"Please, Blaze," she whimpered, her voice raspy with need. "Just fuck me already."

A grin spread across my face at her desperate plea. I loved hearing those words come from her lips. Leaning down, I nipped at her earlobe before whispering in her ear, "Patience, baby girl. We have all night."

Withdrawing my fingers from her slick heat, I positioned myself at her entrance. Her eyes fluttered as I plunged into her, filling her to the brim with the fullness of my cock.

"Goddamn, Blaze." Her whole body quivered as I hit her cervix. "If I'd known you were this well-endowed, I'd have dragged you into a bathroom at the diner and taken you right then and there."

I laughed, the vibrations making us both curse. I couldn't remember the last time I'd laughed during sex. Or, honestly, if it had ever happened. I definitely liked it.

She reached up, tangling her fingers in my hair. "Now, fuck me harder 'cause I promise I won't break."

I grinned. "Yes, ma'am."

I slid my hands down her waist, taking in her curves and binding them around her hips, her breath warm against my skin. I pressed my lips against her neck, and I sank myself into her again, enjoying the feel of her pussy walls squeezing me tighter.

"Fuck, Blaze," she groaned, arching beneath me. "No one's ever made me full like this." Her words emboldened me. With my free hand, I pinched her left nipple, feeling it tighten and harden under my fingertips. I rocked against her, timed to her groans and gasps.

"You like that, huh?"

Her answer was an arch of her back, a whimper that made me smirk. "Yes, Blaze. More."

I gave her nipple a final pinch before grabbing her ass and lifting her against me, slamming in deep.

Trisha's moans grew louder, her body shivering under mine. I moved my hand from her ass to cup her breast, rolling the hard nub in circles, and she cried out. Every thrust was met with a raise of her hips, taking me impossibly deep. Wave after wave of pleasure washed over and through me, each one pushing me closer and closer to the edge.

"Close," she panted. "Kiss me."

"Yes, ma'am." I took her mouth, plundering it with my tongue as I pounded into her.

When she screamed, I swallowed the sound even as I felt her climax explode through her. Her muscles tensed, and the moment her pussy clamped down on me, I was lost. Lost to white-hot ecstasy. Lost in her. Lost in the bliss of feeling strangely at home.

Cleaning up and dropping back into the bed barely registered. Only the woman curling up in my arms and then the soft darkness of my first entirely peaceful sleep in a long time.

# SIX

## *TRISHA*

When I opened my eyes the next morning, I couldn't decide whether my strange surroundings or the gorgeous naked man next to me—both of us sans pajamas—was more mind-boggling. A dull throb between my legs brought back memories of the night before, and I let out a contented sigh.

He'd definitely lived up to my fantasies in bed and then some. My body felt incredible, and I wondered if I'd ever experienced such an intense orgasm before. My previous lovers clearly couldn't hold a candle to this guy.

As his body tensed behind me—not the part currently pressing against my backside—I knew he was awake. I rolled over and felt the bed dip as he hastily exited. I glimpsed his tight ass, still bearing the half-moon imprints my nails had left before he vanished into the bathroom.

Beaming, I propped myself against the pillows, the covers shielding my breasts, and waited. Moments later, he emerged and started getting dressed, avoiding eye contact.

"Bathroom's free," he stated redundantly, his words reflecting his discomfort.

"I can see that." I let my amusement color my words. "You're freaking out, aren't you?"

"No." His eyes darted to my face, and he flushed. "Maybe."

"Any regrets?" I asked lightly, but the unease churning in my stomach betrayed how much his answer mattered to me.

He ruffled his hair, the other hand fumbling with the remote as if unsure of how to proceed. "It's just...I haven't had to deal with a 'morning after' talk in a while."

"Oh, I see. You're the 'love 'em and leave 'em' type," I teased.

His gaze snapped to mine, eyes widening. "What?"

Laughter spilled out of me as I slipped out of bed, holding the sheet up. "Calm down," I reassured him.

"We had a good time, but I'm not after a ring. I'm not even after a date."

Relief shone on his face. "Sorry. I didn't mean to get weird."

"I get it. Neither of us knew how things would turn out. Now that we've cleared up that we're just having fun..." I walked toward him and stopped, looking at him as I released the sheet.

I watched his mouth drop as I strolled past him and into the bathroom, leaving him to think about it. He seemed to have collected himself when I came out, fully dressed. The intense look in his eyes as they swept over me from head to toe spoke volumes.

As I gazed out the window, I saw the snow had stopped. The clear parking lot and road meant we'd have no problems leaving. I pushed aside a twinge of disappointment at not being snowed in with my new friend, imagining all the fun ways we could have spent the time stuck together.

We stepped into the elevator, its doors sliding shut like a curtain closing on our intimate moment above. In the confined space, there was nothing to distract us from each other - just two strangers who shared an undeniable connection. Heavy with anticipation, our breaths mingled in the air as we sank towards the lobby. There was an unsaid energy between us, an electrifying current that promised something extraordinary beyond these walls. This wouldn't end simply because we were stepping back into the real world. No, what happened in that hotel room felt bigger than we would ever admit.

After grabbing coffee and some tempting blueberry muffins from a drive-thru, Blaze merged back onto the highway.

We had been driving for about twenty minutes when I noticed he kept sneaking peeks at me as if he wanted to speak but couldn't find the right words.

"Spit it out," I encouraged.

"Do you..." He paused, then continued. "Do you do this kind of thing a lot?"

My eyebrows went up.

"Damn. That didn't come out right," he quickly added. "I'm not one of those guys who judge women for hooking up or having one-night stands, thinking it's only okay for men. I'm just curious if..."

"If I always sleep with guys who bring me to cheap motel rooms?" I kept my tone mild, even though I wasn't annoyed. I felt Blaze might not be as relaxed about us having slept together as I was.

"Dammit. That really does sound awful, doesn't it?" He rubbed the back of his neck.

A laugh broke from me. "Relax, I get it. And no, this isn't a regular gig for me. You're an exception."

"Is that so?" His chuckle that followed had a tinge of blush to it, and I could tell he dug being special.

And damn if I didn't dig his digging.

"How about we avoid comparing our body counts?" I suggested.

"Deal," he replied with a laugh. "Besides, I've lost count anyway."

"That many conquests? Or too many drunken hookups to remember clearly?"

"Neither. Just spread out over too many years."

I eyed him skeptically. "Okay, Grandpa, so how old are you really?"

"Thirty-five," he side-eyed me. "Please don't say you're nineteen."

"Not yet," I deadpanned. I let the horror fill his face before bursting into laughter. "Kidding! I'm twenty-nine."

He sighed, relieved. "Jeez, Trisha, don't scare me like that."

"You should have seen the look on your face." I smacked his arm with the back of my hand, then realized what I'd done and clapped a hand over my mouth. "Shit, I'm sorry. I do that sometimes."

"You know you're mumbling into your palm, right?"

I lowered my hand, grinning sheepishly. "Apologies. I never quite mastered the art of not talking with a full mouth, either."

My heart pounded as his gaze shifted to my lips, a dark intensity in his eyes. Oh, damn. What had I just uttered? I could have felt embarrassed or even humiliated, but instead, my mind conjured an overwhelming desire for his enormous cock in my mouth. It was an impossible feat, but the thought of attempting it thrilled me.

The desire lingered as we drove through Grand Junction and got closer to Utah. Even the scenic mountains we passed by couldn't shake the thought from my mind.

Discovering that part of Route 70 was called Dinosaur Diamond Prehistoric Highway managed to distract me for a little while, but that would've distracted anyone from anything.

We drove, swapping driving shifts and occasionally grabbing food, but without lingering anywhere for long. Traffic slowed us in the larger cities and in the mountains, and we agreed to drive through the night. Though I doubted it, we both claimed to have slept enough at the hotel. Our sleep had been sound but short. So we drove onward.

When we approached Reno, we both needed to stretch our legs and move around. Because of the weather and traffic in California, the drive from Reno to San Ramon would likely take closer to five or six hours instead of the usual four, but we wanted to press on.

I was eager to see my dad and end the endless driving, yet some of me hesitated to part ways with Blaze. Not after our deep conversations. And certainly not before addressing the burning desire that had been nagging at me since I woke up beside a naked, aroused Blaze. This desire for a repeat had intensified with each passing moment together. Subtle touches, suggestive remarks, and playful banter permeated our conversations, stoking a smoldering tension between us. I needed that tension to explode before we went our separate ways.

The moment I saw the giant Christmas tree in front of a garishly decorated restaurant, an idea struck.

"Let's eat there," I suggested.

"Seriously? That's what you pick?"

I shrugged as I made the turn. "It seems like a lot of fun."

"I offered to treat you to a fancy restaurant, and you instead choose that? It looks like a Hallmark movie threw up on a kid-themed restaurant."

"We can get photos with Santa." I beamed at him. "Come on, from what you've told me about your family, don't you think they'd love to see you in pictures with Santa Claus?"

"I think they'd spend the whole holiday asking if I was on the naughty list."

I glanced at him, letting warmth fill my tone. "Are you?"

I sensed his gaze on me as I pulled into an empty parking spot, but he remained silent until I turned off the engine.

"I guess you'll have to find out," he said with a wicked smile.

The air thickened between us until I thought he'd kiss me, pull me onto his lap, and take me right there in the front seat of the rental. Instead, he reached into the back and surprised me by pulling out the Santa hat the waitress at the diner had made him wear.

"Okay, we'll eat here, but only if *you* wear the hat this time."

I took it from him and put it on. "Let's go."

As Blaze sidled up, I made a snap decision and snatched his hand, weaving my fingers through his. He flinched but didn't retreat.

"So you're one of those Christmas nuts, huh?" Blaze quipped. "Don't tell me your place lights up like a damn UFO landing pad."

"No such luck. I'm in an apartment," I shot back.

"But my tree's up so long it practically earns rent—from Halloween to Valentine's."

"That's... intense."

I flashed a grin as he held the door. "Ease up, Scrooge."

A blast of Christmas music met us at the entrance, making me do a cheerful little skip. Blaze laughed, so I did it again. The family ahead of us in line gave me a look, but I didn't care. I was too busy taking in all the Christmas decorations. The tree outside hadn't prepared me for the wonderland inside.

Plastic elves, three feet tall and sporting hats with bells on their green shoes, lined the area. Every one of Santa's reindeer was on display, Rudolph's oversized red nose shining brightly. Snowmen families greeted visitors with a gentle wave, while a gingerbread house appeared to leap out of the Hansel and Gretel storybook.

"How many?" The hostess's voice drew my attention to her.

"Two," Blaze said, giving her a charming smile.

She did a double-take, her eyes widening. The gaze flicked to me, and her cheeks turned pink.

"Right this way."

After we ordered, the server said we could explore the Christmas Village, and they would page us when our food was ready. Blaze looked doubtful, but I pulled him from his chair and onto the snowflake-decorated path.

"No way," he protested, realizing my plan. "I'm not posing with Santa."

"I'll make it worth your time," I said, placing our photo order with the cameraman.

Soon, Blaze and I flanked Santa's chair as Santa himself grinned for the camera. After several shots, Santa stood up and motioned for Blaze to sit down. Blaze gave me a resigned glance and took the seat. When I perched on his lap, Blaze wrapped his arms around me, and I settled back into his embrace.

Leaning in, I breathed a promise. "Stick with me through this, and I'll make it the prelude to your wildest fantasies."

A spark of interest replaced his skepticism, grip firming suggestively.

My voice dropped to a sultry murmur. "Imagine this as foreplay to the main event - dessert served up hot and early."

His response was immediate, a hardening truth pressing against me. As soon as the flash faded, I sprang up with a grin of thanks, the photographer's assurances about swift delivery barely registering. My focus was singular - scouting the perfect nook to make good on my tantalizing tease.

Exiting the Christmas Village, I veered left instead

of returning to the dining room. Moments later, I noticed an "Employees Only" door. I tried the knob, and it was unlocked. Without pausing to consider the wisdom of my actions, I opened the door and reached for the pull cord of the overhead light. A dim bulb illuminated the supply closet, but the shadows were inconsequential to me. My only concern was if Blaze had closed the door behind him.

Blaze reached for me, but I dropped to my knees, fully aware that if he kissed me, I'd be lost. I couldn't let that happen when I was so close to my goal. I didn't care about the consequence of damp panties and a throbbing ache between my legs for the rest of the evening. Having him in my mouth was all that mattered.

"Trisha."

"Hush," I ordered, reaching for his waistband. "We've got to hurry."

I tugged his jeans to mid-thigh and then pulled down his boxer briefs to find him already mostly hard. He groaned as I wrapped my fingers around his base, stroking him from root to tip. Looking up at him through my lashes, I ran my tongue around his head.

"Don't hold back," I told him. "I want you to come in my mouth."

"Fuck, Trisha." He reached out to touch my cheek.

"I've wanted to taste you for too long," I told him. "Think of it as my Christmas present."

And with that comment, I wrapped my lips around the head of his cock and applied suction, moving down as quickly as I could. My hand came up as I went until lips met fingers. I couldn't take all of him, no matter how much time I had, but I knew what to do with what I couldn't reach.

His skin was velvet soft under my palm, just as I remembered, and as he slid over my tongue, I tasted the tang of salt and his own flavor. The weight of him made heat coil in my stomach, but the sounds he made were what had arousal spiking hot and hard. He cursed and groaned, his hand tangling in my hair. All sorts of words spilled from his lips, coming faster and more garbled as I increased the pressure of my mouth and my hand. Working them in tandem, I pushed him hard and fast to the edge. When his hips jerked, his muscles tensing under the hand I had steadying me on his thigh, I knew he was close. I didn't stop, didn't even pause to draw things out, to make him beg for release. I liked that idea, but we didn't have the time.

I set my teeth against his soft skin, just enough to send him tumbling into the abyss. His cock swelled in my mouth, salty liquid spilling across my tongue and down my throat. I held him to me as I swallowed it all, reveling in how he kept saying my name. Only after he stopped coming did I let his softening shaft slip from between my lips.

I sat back on my heels and looked up at him, knowing that, no matter what else happened this year, this would be the memory I'd take with me into the next.

Merry Christmas to me.

# SEVEN

## *BLAZE*

I insisted on driving the last stretch, claiming it was because I knew the area near my parent's home, but in truth, it was because I couldn't trust my hands to stay still if I wasn't holding the steering wheel. Hell, I'd been half-ready to senselessly have sex with her when we got back in the car after dinner. Or maybe just make her orgasm on my tongue to repay what she'd done in that closet.

Women had gone down on me before, but none had ever compared to this woman, to what she'd done to me, for me. The chemistry between us was unlike anything I'd ever felt. Absolutely insane. Despite my eagerness to be done with the drive, another part of me wasn't even near ready to say goodbye to Trisha.

But wishing wouldn't change anything. We both had family waiting for us and lives to return to. Even though that blowjob would stay with me forever.

As we neared San Ramon, we talked less, cherishing these last moments alone. I steered into my parents' driveway late at night, harboring a plan to offer something I believed we both desired—more time.

"Wow, this is where you grew up?" Trisha asked, eyes wide as I parked in front of the massive house Patrick had built for his blended family. "Or, sorry. I meant, in your teens–"

"Don't worry," I said soothingly. "As you know, my family background is very confusing. You should've been there when my step-sister, London, had to create a family tree for school." I switched off the engine and turned to face her. Meeting Trisha's inquisitive gaze, I nearly gave in to the temptation to kiss her. Though reason prevailed. Getting caught making out with a woman in the car, especially while about to make her a proposition, was unwise.

"It's pretty late," I began. "And I know San Francisco isn't that far away, but we've been in the car for a long time."

A smile played about her lips. "Are you worried about me driving by myself?"

"Yeah," I admitted. "I know you're a good driver,

but look at how bad the traffic was the last fifty miles here."

"It was pretty bad," she agreed. "And I am tired."

A wave of relief washed over me. I couldn't quite tell whether she really didn't want to drive that night or was just following my lead and not ready to diverge just yet.

"How about you crash here for the night?" I ventured, praying my casual tone masked my racing heart. "It's no biggie, and you'll snag a solid night's sleep. You'll hit your dad's place bright-eyed tomorrow morning for the holiday."

Her smile warmed the chilly night as her fingers brushed mine. "I'd love to. And thanks... for giving a damn."

A light came on inside. I let out a breath. "Time to go in."

We picked up our belongings and made our way to the front door. Halfway there, the door swung open to reveal my cousin, Paris, a petite, curvy woman with jet-black hair tied back in a ponytail.

"Finally, you're here, Blaze," she said, hugging herself. "Hurry up. I'm at the best part of my book."

She looked surprised when she noticed the woman with me, but Paris held back any sarcastic remarks, showing remarkable restraint.

"Trisha, meet my cousin, Paris Carideo," I introduced as we approached. "Paris, this is Trisha Easton, my... well, travel buddy."

Trisha chuckled. "I appreciate that title. It sounds sophisticated, not like someone he just met at a car rental in Chicago."

A gleam appeared in Paris's eyes. "I like her."

"She's headed to see her dad in San Francisco," I said, ignoring Paris's remark. "But we decided it wasn't safe for her to drive alone tonight, so she'll stay here and head out in the morning."

Paris looked from me to Trisha, her smile widening. "Got it. You know where things are, so I'll let you be."

"Seriously?" I asked, locking the door after us. "You're not going to quiz me about our trip?"

"Nope," Paris replied. "I'm about to read a steamy scene where a werewolf cowboy sweeps his destined partner off her feet, and I can't wait."

"I'd rather not hear more," I said quickly. "That was already too much TMI."

Paris's smile didn't fade. "I'll pass you the book when I'm done."

I rolled my eyes while Trisha snickered. We trailed after Paris up the stairs, but veered right when she turned left. Trisha was sticking close to me. As everyone else was asleep, the house was silent, requiring us to tread softly. My stomach knotted with anxiety as we approached my bedroom, but I waited until we were standing before the door before uttering a word.

"I'm not sure if the other rooms are set up for guests," I whispered. "I can crash on the couch if you'd rather have the room."

She dismissed the idea with a shake of her head, amusement twinkling in her eyes. "Fuck no. Show me what Blaze Gracen was like as a teenager."

"Don't get your hopes up," I said with a grin. As I pushed open the door, a rush of nostalgia hit me—the walls still boasted the same faded posters of Star Wars and a signed basketball jersey from my high school team. The room hadn't changed much since my teenage years; Aunt Theresa must have thought it sacrilegious to alter it.

Trisha stepped in behind me, her laughter a soft melody. "Oh, you were one of those Star Wars fanatics," she teased, pointing at a dusty Millennium Falcon model on my shelf.

I shrugged, a sheepish grin tugging at my lips. "Guilty as charged. But don't act like you're not impressed by my extensive collection."

Her eyes sparkled as she picked up a bobblehead of Yoda and gave it a flick. "Impressed or worried? There's a fine line between collector and hoarder, Mr. Gracen."

"Hey, I'll have you know each piece here is a classic," I defended, watching her delicate fingers dance over the spines of worn sci-fi novels stacked haphazardly on the bookshelf.

She raised an eyebrow, pulling out a book with an absurdly muscled alien on the cover. "Classic literature? Really?"

I couldn't help but laugh at her mock-serious expression. "It's important to appreciate all forms of storytelling," I said, trying to maintain a semblance of dignity.

Trisha turned around, surveying the room with an impish grin. "So, where does teenage Blaze sit and brood about the universe? On the bed with these superhero sheets?"

Following her gaze to my old bed decked out in comic book bedding—something else Aunt Theresa hadn't changed—I felt heat creep up my neck. "Uh, those are... vintage," I stammered.

"Vintage?" she echoed with a chuckle. "Is that what we're calling it?"

"Let's just say they're from a time when saving the galaxy seemed as simple as putting on a cape," I replied, hoping my voice didn't betray how endearing I found her teasing.

She plopped down on the bed, bouncing slightly on the mattress. "Well then, Captain Blaze," she said with a dramatic flourish, "your mission tonight as my sidekick is to make sure your heroine gets some rest before her last leg tomorrow."

I joined her on the bed, unable to resist the pull of her playful energy. "I'm the sidekick?" I scoffed playfully. "I think you've got our roles reversed."

Trisha winked and laid back against my pillows. "We'll see about that."

A chuckle escaped me, and as I drifted to sleep, the startling thought followed me into the darkness.

We fitted together perfectly.

# EIGHT

## *TRISHA*

This time, waking up with a warm body pressed against me, I knew who I was with, but it took me a moment to figure out where we were. This was not another hotel room; we were at Blaze's family's home. And it was Christmas Eve.

Which meant it was time for me to leave. It was time for Blaze to be with his family and me to be with my dad.

Holding that thought, I carefully slipped from under Blaze's arm without waking him, and tiptoed across the hall to the bathroom, silently praying I wouldn't run into any of his family members. I wasn't afraid to meet them, but aside from Paris, I wasn't sure who else was aware I was here, and sneaking out of Blaze's room was not the first impression I aimed to give.

Escaping undetected, I retrieved my bag, surprised by how torn I was about leaving. On the one hand, I wanted to see my dad, and I was looking forward to our holiday together, but on the other hand, I'd really enjoyed my time with Blaze and knew that once I left, I'd most likely never see him again.

But we'd both made a point of saying that we were just having fun.

I had a feeling that would change if I didn't leave now.

After collecting my things, I sat gently on the bed's edge and texted my dad to say I was leaving San Ramon and would be home soon.

"Hey."

Blaze's voice was low and gravelly, causing an involuntary reaction that made me squeeze my thighs together. I reminded myself not to ogle his impressive, muscled upper body.

"You're getting ready to leave?"

I nodded.

"How about breakfast first?" he asked, propping himself up and allowing the sheets to fall to his waist. "You should eat something before you head out."

"I couldn't," I said, shaking my head.

"Believe me, if you go without letting Aunt Theresa feed you, I'll never hear the end of it," he insisted with a beseeching look. "You'd really be helping me out."

I chuckled. "Okay. Breakfast and coffee, then I'll hit the road. Half hour, sound good?"

"That should work," he replied, tossing the covers aside.

I felt a tinge of disappointment when he pulled on his pants, although they did little to hide the fact that he had a great butt. I watched said butt as he exited the room and then turned my attention back to my phone, ready to inform my dad that I'd be leaving soon and heading straight home.

A reply from Dad popped up before I finished typing my message, and I stopped to read it.

*Have you seen the weather forecast? A big storm is rolling in across the bay this morning, and it'll last all day. I don't want you driving in that. Can you stay somewhere safe?*

I frowned in confusion.

I swiftly checked the weather app, convinced Dad was mistaken. He's always overprotective. There couldn't be a severe storm approaching. How unlucky could one person be?

San Ramon looked safe for now, but glancing at the radar and peering west, I saw Dad was correct.

"Shit," I muttered.

"What's wrong?" Blaze was immediately there, crouching in front of me, an anxious expression on his face. "Are you okay?"

"I'm okay," I reassured him, feeling my heart skip at his concern. "There's a nasty storm rolling in from the bay. Even if I leave now, I'd be caught in it. My dad's worried about me driving through that."

"Just stay here, then."

Blaze made it sound so easy that I looked at him as though he'd suggested something outrageous.

"What?"

He flashed a grin and sat beside me on the bed. "Stay here until the storm's over. It's not a big deal."

I lifted my phone to show him the storm's magnitude. "If I stay, I could be here all day, maybe even overnight."

He gently placed a stray curl behind my ear. "That's okay."

I quirked an eyebrow. "But it's Christmas Eve. I can't just barge in on your family. I'll look for a hotel."

"There's really no burden," he insisted. "Besides, how will you find an available room tonight?"

He was right.

"Thank you," I accepted. "As long as your family doesn't mind, I'll keep to myself and—"

"You're celebrating Christmas Eve with us," he interrupted. "My family will love having you. We're very big on hospitality. Trust me."

"Won't this make things awkward for you?" I bravely voiced my other worry. "I noticed your sister's reaction when she saw me with you last night. Everyone will assume we're a couple, and I'm sure you don't want to spend all day correcting them that nothing is going on."

He smiled. "I wouldn't go as far as to say there's *nothing* going on between us."

"You know what I mean." I playfully hit his arm, trying to ignore the spark I felt when our skin touched. "They'll treat it like you've brought a girl home for the family, even if you explain."

He shrugged. "They might believe us, or they might not. But if it doesn't bother you, it doesn't bother me. And they won't be rude to you. Aunt Theresa will see to that."

"You're okay with your cousins and siblings giving you a hard time?" It could complicate Blaze's Christmas celebrations, and he didn't deserve that.

"To keep you safe," he said, "I'd endure much more than that."

I swallowed hard, losing myself in his captivating

eyes. I had to remind myself that hooking up with Blaze again wasn't why I would stay overnight, but I couldn't deny wanting it.

"Besides," he said dryly, "with every family member here, there's never a holiday without teasing or arguing. It's all in fun. We might have been a bit mean as kids, but we're grown-ups now. We know better."

His casual remarks did little to ease the tension.

"Come on," he said, standing up. He offered his hand. "Let's have breakfast, and I'll introduce you to the early birds. You'll see, there's nothing to worry about."

I reluctantly accepted his hand, intertwining my fingers with his.

Before I even thought about dialing my dad's number to fill him in on my Christmas Eve stay, I figured it was only fitting to double-check with Blaze's aunt and uncle first. I may trust Blaze's invitation, but beyond my brief encounter with Paris, his relatives were strangers to me. He could be off-base about how they'd take the news. Or maybe there was some family drama he wasn't clued into that could throw a wrench in the works.

Steeling myself for the unexpected, I followed Blaze's confident stride down the stairs. The aroma of a home-cooked meal grew stronger as we entered a kitchen where a woman, her hair a striking tapestry of dark reddish-brown threaded with silver, stood attentively over the stove, stirring a pot of something that sent delightful scents wafting through the air.

"Morning," Blaze greeted, guiding us closer before bending to kiss the woman's cheek gently. "I have someone special to introduce to you."

She pivoted our way, her warm brown eyes locking with mine. With a hospitable gesture, she dried her hands on a towel and extended them towards me, her grasp welcoming and firm.

"I'm Theresa Carideo."

"Trisha Easton," I replied, her warmth winning me over instantly. "I hope it's not inconvenient that I'm dropping in on Christmas Eve."

"Absolute nonsense," Theresa dismissed with an easy smile, brushing off my concerns.

Blaze chimed in, "She was planning on heading to San Francisco today."

Theresa's expression shifted to concern. "Oh, dear. You must not have caught the weather updates?"

Blaze nodded. "Her dad wants her to stay put for now," he said. "I told her we wouldn't mind."

"And we don't," Theresa quickly agreed. "Stay as long as you need, dear. More company is always better."

Still hesitant, I asked, "Are you sure?"

Her smile was as warm and welcoming as the one

Paris had given me the night before. "As long as you're here, you're part of the family. Now, go fill your plate before everyone else gets here, and it's all gone."

With a thankful smile, I released Blaze's hand and headed to the pile of plates Theresa pointed out. "Thank you, I definitely will!"

## NINE

*BLAZE*

The weather had certainly played its part, turning what was usually a bustling Christmas Eve gathering at Theresa and Patrick's into a more intimate family affair. But if there was one thing that remained unaffected by the whims of nature, it was Theresa's boundless enthusiasm for the holiday season. Her love for Christmas infused every corner of the house, making the atmosphere as festive and lively as ever.

Dressing up was non-negotiable in the Gracen family traditions, even with the guest list cut in half. I found myself in charcoal gray dress pants and a crisp white button-down shirt, the platinum cufflinks—gifted by Theresa and Patrick two years prior—gleaming at my wrists. The initials of my late parents etched into them always served as a gentle reminder of their presence, making me wonder what they would've thought of our lives now. The thought of Trisha crossed my mind, igniting a mix of anticipation and curiosity about their would-be impression of her.

As I stepped out of my room, the sight of Trisha emerging from the guest room abruptly interrupted my musings. Time seemed to slow for a moment as I took her in. She was a vision in the dress borrowed from Paris, the deep red fabric complementing her fair skin, making it glow under the soft lighting of the hallway. The dress was a perfect amalgamation of elegance and allure, clinging to her in all the right places, modest yet tantalizing with its thigh-high slit.

Her heels gave her height, bringing her eyes to meet mine, sparking a connection that felt electric even from a distance. The desire to close that distance, to taste the promise that lingered in her gaze, was almost overwhelming.

"Blaze, stop drooling over your new girlfriend and get your ass downstairs. Chow time!" Xander's voice, laced with brotherly irreverence, broke the spell. He shot us an amused glance before sauntering off towards the stairs.

So, no kissing.

Yet.

I extended my arm to Trisha, infusing the gesture

with a mix of formality and warmth. "My apologies for Xander," I said with a half-smirk. "He's still battling jetlag. Living in England has him on a completely different clock." As I looked at her, I couldn't help but add, "By the way, you look absolutely stunning tonight."

Trisha linked her arm with mine, her cheeks tinged with a soft blush as her eyes met mine. "Well, you both look dashing despite the time differences. And England, huh? What's the story there?"

"He's a soccer player," I replied, my voice carrying a hint of pride as we reached the foot of the stairs.

Uncle Patrick, overhearing our conversation, couldn't resist adding his two cents with a chuckle. "It's called football, lad." He shook his head, his light blue eyes twinkling. "Have I taught you nothing?" He took Trisha's free hand and brushed his lips across her knuckles. "You look lovely, lass."

"Thank you," Trisha said, her cheeks turning pink. "And thank you for letting me join your family's Christmas."

Patrick waved off her thanks with a warm grin. "Oh, we're always happy to have more around the table. The more the merrier, as I like to say."

As we made our way to the dining room, my sister Rose caught my eye. Her usual ranch attire was replaced with an elegant black dress accentuating her natural beauty. She stood out in stark contrast to her usual rugged, outdoorsy look.

"Hey, Rose," I said, unable to hide my surprise. "You clean up pretty good, huh?"

Rose rolled her eyes playfully. "Don't act so shocked, big brother. I do own something other than jeans and flannel shirts, you know."

Trisha giggled beside me, and Rose shot her a conspiratorial wink. "Don't let him fool you, Trisha. He's just scared I'll outshine him tonight."

Rose's grimace as she adjusted her dress was fleeting, replaced quickly by a warm smile directed at Trisha. "Hey, thanks for carting my brother back here. We kinda like having him around for Christmas."

"Yeah, who else is gonna inhale Mom's quiche?" A blinding smile flashed against my cousin Rome's sun-kissed skin. "Yo, Trisha, right? We haven't formally met." He inched closer, dropping his voice. "Wanna sneak off and make some mistletoe magic? A little Christmas cheer, if you know what I mean?"

"Rome," I warned.

He shrugged, his mischievous gaze twinkling. "What? I heard she's not your official girlfriend or anything."

Trisha shot back with a smirk, unfazed by my cousin's towering height. "Nice try, Romeo, but I'll pass. Kudos for the effort, though."

I nudged her gently towards the dining room. "Come on, let's attack the buffet before Rome here eats everything."

Trisha's eyes widened as we entered the dining room, taking in the vast spread. "Holy smokes, that's what you call a buffet? It's like Thanksgiving on steroids!"

I laughed. "Yep, and everyone leaves with enough leftovers to last till New Year's. Aunt Theresa's pretty generous with the to-go boxes."

Trisha eyed the food like it was the eighth wonder of the world. "Forget playing it cool. I'm diving in. This is some serious food temptation."

As we filled our plates, Theresa and Patrick settled into their usual spots, the heart and soul of the family. Paris, Rome, Xander, and Rose followed suit, with London and her fiancé, Spencer, joining last, their baby son Alexander snoozing peacefully in his arms.

Aunt Theresa's tender gaze on her grandson sent a wave of nostalgia through me, a bittersweet reminder of what could have been. My fingers brushed over the cufflinks, the engravings a tangible connection to my parents, and I felt a twinge of sadness at the thought that they would never meet their grandchildren.

"Hey," Trisha nudged me, "you okay?"

I shook off the melancholy, squeezing her hand

with a reassuring smile. "Yeah, I'm good. Just a moment of nostalgia."

She searched my face, her eyes a mirror of empathy, but before she could delve deeper, Patrick's booming voice called everyone to attention. His annual Christmas Eve speech was always a highlight, filled with gratitude and a bit of humor. This year, he kept it short and sweet, much to everyone's amusement. "For the kids," he claimed, though we all knew his stomach was the real driving force.

Trisha and I joined the line to load up our plates, the spread an impressive array of flavors and aromas. "You've got to try these crab puffs," I recommended, adding a few to her plate. "And don't miss the Scottish specialties. Aunt Theresa outdoes herself every year."

WITH PLATES FULL, we found a cozy spot in the living room, surrounded by the hum of family conversations. "I'll be right back with the eggnog," I told her, slipping away to the kitchen.

There, I poured two cups of Aunt Theresa's famous eggnog—the version with a generous splash of rum. The memory of my younger cousins trying to sneak sips of the adults' eggnog brought a grin to my face.

As I rejoined Trisha in the living room, handing

her the spiced eggnog, I caught the tail end of her conversation with London. They were discussing the delicate balance of career and family. Trisha listened intently, her eyes reflecting genuine interest.

"You've got an incredible talent, London," Trisha encouraged. "Balancing motherhood and a career must be tough, but you've got this."

London's face lit up with gratitude. "Thanks, Trisha. And hey, if you're ever in the area when I'm performing, I insist you come see the show."

Trisha's modesty was evident as she hesitated. "I wouldn't want to impose..."

"Nonsense," Spencer interjected warmly. "We'd be thrilled to have you. Consider it an open invitation."

As they continued their conversation, Rome sidled up to me, his curiosity piqued. "So, Blaze, you really just bumped into her at the airport and decided to go on a cross-country road trip? Just like that?"

I nodded, sipping my eggnog. "That's how it happened."

Rome's eyes flicked towards Trisha, a mischievous glint in them. "She's quite a catch, huh?"

He was more teasing than anything, but I felt a protective surge. "She's more than just pretty, Rome. She's got brains and a wicked sense of humor that could put most comedians to shame."

He held up his hands in mock surrender. "Easy,

cousin. I get it. She's great. You don't need to sell me on her."

Just as I was about to comment, Trisha's voice cut through. "Wait, London. You're telling me this serious, buttoned-up brother of yours used to dance around in his underwear, lip-syncing boy band songs into his hairbrush during high school?" Trisha's eyes sparkled with amusement as she regarded me.

I felt my face grow warm. Of all the things for London to reveal...

"Oh yeah, he was quite the entertainer," London said, clearly enjoying my discomfort. "There's probably still video evidence somewhere. I'll have to do some digging when I'm back in New York."

"Don't you dare," I warned, trying to keep my tone light despite my mortification.

"What? It's adorable," Trisha teased. "I'd pay good money to see Blaze Gracen rocking out in his briefs."

"He probably still does it but keeps it to himself," Rose joined in, unable to resist the chance to tease me. "Once a rockstar, always a rockstar, right?"

"Alright, alright, let's change the subject," I pleaded, though I was smiling too. Their playful banter reminded me of old times when we were kids together, well before we'd scattered across the country.

"Sorry, but you brought this on yourself when you decided to drive halfway across the country with a total stranger," London said. "We need to give Trisha the full Blaze Gracen experience so she knows what she's gotten herself into."

"Speaking of which, has he told you about the time he-" Rose started.

"Okay!" I cut in. "How about we talk about something else now? Preferably not related to my most embarrassing moments?"

The girls laughed, clearly enjoying this rare chance to team up on me. But as mortified as I was, there was something nice about it, too. Having Trisha here, interacting so easily with my family...it just felt right, like she belonged.

As the hour grew late, Spencer and London returned to their room, prompting the rest of us to begin tidying up. My aunt and I assured Trisha she didn't need to assist us, but she was adamant. I noticed Aunt Theresa's approving gaze as she thanked Trisha.

Soon, Trisha and I became the last two left downstairs. We were both dusting off crumbs from the floor when we looked up and realized we were standing under a sprig of mistletoe hanging from the archway leading to the living room.

"I guess we have to," Trisha teased, her voice as warm as the longing in her eyes. "Mistletoe calls for a kiss. Those are the rules."

"We can't go breaking the rules," I replied.

"We might end up on the naughty list if we do."

I leaned closer, and when my lips were a breath away from hers, I said, "Trust me, with what I was thinking the moment I saw you in that dress, I'm already on the list."

And then my mouth covered hers, and she was all I knew, along with the taste of cinnamon and chocolate, as my tongue slid into her mouth. Her soft moan sent a rush of arousal through me, and I barely managed to keep from deepening the kiss into something that'd be indecent for the middle of a house full of people upstairs. As I raised my head, I let her see I wasn't done with her yet.

When she nodded, I took her hand and led her up the stairs and to the guest room that Theresa had prepared for Trisha. I had considered having Trisha stay in my room, but since I'd been telling everyone we weren't together, it would only raise questions I wasn't ready to answer.

So she was sleeping apart from me tonight.

I couldn't bear to leave her at the door. If she asked me in, I'd go. I craved more than just that mistletoe kiss. In fact, since our encounter at the motel, I'd been thinking about how and when I could make love to her again.

She opened the door to the guest room and tightened her hold on my hand, a questioning look on her face. In answer, I followed her into the room and closed the door behind me. Her mouth found mine even as we stumbled toward the bed, the electricity racing across my veins, making it difficult for me to think clearly.

When the backs of her legs hit the bed, I caught her wrists and broke the kiss. With my eyes locked on hers, I nudged her until she sat down on the edge of the bed. I kept my gaze on her face as I fell to my knees.

"I would love nothing more than to peel that dress off of you and take you right here," I said as I slid my hands up her legs, slowly moving up her calves to her knees and then to her thighs. Her breathing hitched when my fingers inched under the hem of her dress. "But I don't think that'd be a good idea with my aunt and uncle sleeping next door."

She opened her mouth to protest but instead sucked in a breath as I pushed up her dress, exposing a pair of black cotton panties.

"But don't worry, sweetheart. I'm not going to leave you frustrated."

Her knees parted, and I leaned down to press a kiss to the inside of her thigh. She made a soft sound that went straight to my cock. I ignored the erection, starting to press against the front of my pants, and focused instead on the woman in front of me.

"You've had me in your mouth," I continued, "and now it's my turn to taste you."

I pulled aside the damp fabric hiding her from me and ran my tongue along her slit. She groaned, her legs falling further apart and opening her up more to me.

She reached out and put her hand on my head, tugging me toward her, and I wasted no time burying my face between her legs.

She cried out, but a pillow muffled the sound, so I didn't pause. My tongue slid between her folds, circling her entrance before dipping into her core. I didn't linger there, instead moving up to her clit and teasing that swollen bundle of nerves. Remembering what she'd liked with my fingers, I mimicked the movements with my tongue, making quick back-and-forth motions across the top.

She was panting heavily, quivering with excitement. Her scent was intoxicating, a mix of her feminine heat and the faint aroma of her soap hitting my senses. Her fingers tangled in my hair, urging me on as I lapped at her folds and teased her clit. With swift flicks of my tongue, I sent vibrations through her sensitive nerves.

I sucked on her clit, starting with mild suction, feeling the vibrant sensation of her quivering feminine flesh in my mouth. As she moaned and hissed, I increased the suction, making it harder, pulling tighter, and sliding my tongue across her swollen bud in long, slow strokes while pressing my lips tight around it.

As I lapped at her center, my tongue found her sensitive bud again and again as she groaned and gasped. Her scent grew stronger with every spasm, her taste becoming my own. The pillow muffled each moan, so I wasn't too concerned about anybody hearing us.

My free hand found her entrance, and I slipped a finger inside her hot, tight channel. With each tongue thrust, I plunged deeper, adding a second finger, stretching her as she whimpered. She tasted like heaven on my tongue, and I savored the tangy, salty mix of her essence against the roof of my mouth.

Watching my fingers disappear into her core made my cock hard as a rock. I saw she was close, but I couldn't stop. How could I? Not when her moans were a symphony to my ears, a soundtrack that caught me completely? I felt her inner walls pulse and shudder with desire, and I grew more insistent, suctioning harder on that bud while my fingers pistoned in and out of her tight, wet pussy.

Trisha's breathing became more ragged as I prepared her body to clamber over the edge, her fingernails digging into my scalp and her hips thrusting against my face as her legs splayed, giving me better access to her tight channel. She was so close. I could feel it in the way her core pulsed in perfect rhythm with my fingers as they mimicked the actions of my tongue.

She shrieked, jerking under my ministrations as her legs trembled. I held on, riding the wave with her, enjoying the capsize of her senses. It was all I could do to let her ride out her orgasm, bathing in her ecstasy, tasting it, and feeling it course down my throat.

As she subsided, I lifted my head, my eyes locked on hers, her face a vision of satisfaction and, dare I say, relief.

"Blaze," she breathed, eyes dark with desire. She scooted closer, nestling into my chest, taking long, shuddery breaths. "That was...that was incredible." I kissed her forehead, biting back my need, the weight of her head on my shoulder grounding me in reality.

Her fingers traced circles on my chest, sending little sparks dancing across my skin. And while my body ached with unfulfilled needs, I knew that tonight wasn't about us having sex - it was about showing her that I cared enough to give her pleasure without expecting anything in return.

Without thinking, my arm snaked around her waist, holding her close. She shifted slightly, bringing herself flush against me, her curves fitting perfectly against mine. There was something comforting about her warmth, the feel of her heartbeat pressed against mine. It was like coming home after a long journey, finally settling into the place where I belonged.

For a moment, I allowed myself to imagine what it might be like to share a future with her, to wake up every morning with her by my side, her hair splayed across the pillow as the early morning light caressed her sleeping face. To shuffle to the kitchen together, bleary-eyed, as the coffee brewed, wrapping my arms around her waist and planting a soft kiss on her temple. To come home after a long day and find her curled up on the couch, a contented smile lighting up her features when she saw me walk through the door. To climb into bed each night and pull her close, listening to her steady breathing as she drifted off to sleep, knowing she was safe and happy.

But the idea was foolish. I barely knew her. Despite the connection I felt, the sense that I had known her for far longer than I actually had, she was still practically a stranger. So, I pushed those thoughts aside, concentrating on the present moment.

What the hell was this woman doing to me?

# TEN

## *TRISHA*

Morning light crept through the curtains as I stirred awake, instinctively reaching for a warmth that wasn't there. The absence left a hollow feeling, like missing a step in the dark. As I lay there, eyes still heavy with sleep, last night's memories came crashing in, each one sending a thrilling shiver down my spine like a mischievous whisper.

I rolled onto my side, staring up at the ceiling fan. Its blades cut through the air with unhurried grace, reminding me how a single, spontaneous decision could set life spinning in an entirely new direction. Just a couple of days ago, offering Blaze a ride was a simple choice, a spark ignited by a bit of chemistry and the prospect of some fun on a tedious drive. But now, it felt like I had opened a door to a room I never knew existed, filled with unexpected emotions and possibilities.

I glanced at the clock. Early morning, still. But the scent of cinnamon and bacon was wafting through the air, a sure sign that the day was already in full swing for someone. Blaze had told me that Christmas morning at the McCraes was a big deal; a tradition steeped in the kind of familial warmth you read about in holiday novels. Yesterday, Paris had mentioned wearing pajamas for breakfast, even offering to lend me some if my wardrobe was lacking. I'd laughed it off, telling her I was all set. My usual comfy sleepwear was back in New York, but luckily, I'd packed my festive, Christmas-themed PJs for this trip.

As I sauntered into the kitchen, I saw that I'd nailed the dress code. The place was a riot of holiday cheer, with everyone sporting Christmas attire. Even the baby was dolled up like a cute, chubby snowman.

"Trisha wins," Paris declared with a grin as I made my grand entrance. "Sorry, little man. The snowman is cute, but her pajamas rock."

I gave them all a playful twirl, showing off the reindeer playing various sports on my pajamas. "See? Basketball, baseball, football..." I caught Patrick's eye. "Both kinds of football," I added with a wink.

Patrick laughed, giving me this approving nod.

"She's quicker on the uptake than you lot," he said to his family, his smile easy and warm.

Then Blaze walked in, and I swear, my heart must've skipped a beat or two. "Morning," I managed, feeling this goofy smile spread across my face. "Merry Christmas."

He smiled, returned the greeting, and gestured to the table laden with food. "Let's eat before this lot clears it out."

Xander, piling his plate with scrambled eggs, chimed in. "Like we'd ever let that happen. Mom cooks for an army."

"Don't pretend that you won't be sneaking down here at midnight to finish off the bacon," Paris pointed a fork at him.

"One time!" he protested. "I only did that one time."

She raised her eyebrows.

"It was Sean all those other times."

"Sean is Xander's identical twin," Paris explained as I took the seat between her and Blaze. "Half the time, even we can't tell them apart, and they enjoy using that to their advantage."

"Like you wouldn't do the same thing if you had a twin," Xander said, snatching a piece of bacon from Paris's plate.

"Mom!"

"Xander McCrae, you stop that," Theresa scolded, a twinkle in her eye and amusement in her voice. "The next batch is almost ready. Eat your eggs."

The chitchat flew back and forth, light and easy, and I soaked it all in, happily munching on Theresa's heavenly cinnamon rolls. Watching and listening to them was like being inside a warm, loving whirlwind. Blaze, especially, seemed different here, more open and relaxed. I couldn't decide what was more distracting—his infectious laugh or how his t-shirt clung just right.

But then Theresa's voice cut through the chatter, bringing us back to the present. "Dishes in the dishwasher, everyone. We've got more family coming soon."

Right, more people. This already bustling, lively group was just the tip of the iceberg.

Paris and I retreated to the kitchen. "You good with clothes for today?" she asked, her tone casual but caring.

I nodded. "I am, thanks. And thank you for lending me the dress last night."

"You're welcome." Paris's smile was warm. "Blaze seemed to like it."

Heat flooded my face. "Paris, it's not like—"

"I know," she said, waving her hand dismissively. "You both say you're not involved. But I see the way you two look at each other. Those aren't the looks of people who're just random travel buddies."

Paris was right; Blaze and I had an undeniable chemistry, even if neither of us dared put a label on it. Back in my room, her words lingered in my mind as I swapped my reindeer pajamas for black jeans and a soft green sweater. I carefully ran my fingers through my curls, trying to tame them into something presentable, then dabbed on just enough makeup to look fresh. I kept telling myself it was all in the spirit of Christmas, not because I wanted to catch Blaze's eye. But deep down, I knew better.

As I descended the stairs, the sound of the front door opening and the buzz of unfamiliar voices pulled me towards the entrance. A towering man stood, easily over six feet tall, with golden blond hair that seemed to capture the room's light. He was embracing London warmly, his presence commanding yet gentle. Beside him stood a dark-haired girl with strikingly bright blue eyes, her gaze fixed affectionately on the baby.

Two more figures entered - one woman, exuding a maternal warmth as she hugged Theresa, and a teenage girl, who seemed slightly withdrawn, perhaps unsure of her place in this sprawling family scene.

I knew that feeling all too well.

Before I could process more, Blaze was by my side, his presence instantly comforting. He began making introductions. "This is Alec McCrae, his wife Lumen, and their daughters, Soleil and Evanne."

My head spun as the house filled with more people and introductions. Some names I recognized from Blaze's stories, others were new. The McCrae family gathering was like a kaleidoscope of personalities and stories, each one more fascinating than the last.

Xander's twin, Sean, the motivational speaker with a magnetic presence, walked in, followed by the whisky maker Brody McCrae and his wife, Freedom, alongside their child. Eoin McCrae and his wife, Aline, Freedom's sister, added to the eclectic mix.

Then there was Blaze's brother, Fury, arriving alongside Cory McCrae, known for their success in Palo Alto's financial sector. Cory's twin brother, Carson McCrae, appeared with his fiancé, Vix Teal. Their names were familiar, especially after Carson's headline-making fashion show.

Maggie McCrae, a renowned violinist from New York, entered with her husband, Drake, and their twins. The loving way Drake looked at her and their children spoke volumes about their relationship.

Behind them, Andrea Locke, a diminutive woman with striking jet-black hair and dark gray eyes that seemed to absorb the light around her, added an enigmatic presence to the gathering. Andrea, like me, was a stray in this sea of familial bonds, brought together by the magnetic pull of the McCrae clan.

London whispered Andrea was Blaze's high school crush. This news blindsided me. A pang of discomfort twisted my stomach, and my smile froze momentarily.

*Stop it!*

I reminded myself that I was only here until the roads were safe to travel again.

But little did it help stop the flare of irrational jealousy I felt as I watched Blaze hug Andrea.

He was just being polite; I knew that. Still, I couldn't shake the sudden, ridiculous urge to stake some kind of claim.

Before I could act on that foolish impulse, I felt a gentle hand on my arm.

"Hey, you okay?" It was London, her expression softly understanding.

I nodded, trying to play it cool. "Yeah, of course! Just a lot going on with everyone arriving."

London smiled, a knowing look in her eyes. "It's a lot, for sure. Especially when you're not used to our crazy clan." She lowered her voice conspiratorially. "Between you and me, I think my brother's pretty smitten with you. So don't worry about Andrea. She's ancient history."

I laughed, feeling myself relax. "Good to know."

Impulsively, I pulled London into a quick hug. "Thanks," I whispered.

"Anytime," she whispered back.

Across the room, Blaze caught my eye, giving me a private little smile before getting drawn back into conversation with one of his nieces.

I hoped London was right. Whatever history Blaze had with Andrea, it seemed to be far in the past. And the way he kept glancing my way, as if to ensure I was okay, told me everything I needed to know.

But deep down, a small voice wondered: If Blaze still harbored feelings for Andrea, where would that leave us? The thought was unsettling, but I resolved not to let it dampen the festive spirit. After all, I was here to enjoy Christmas, not to get entangled in what might have been. I took a deep breath, ready to navigate the complexities of the day with a smile, determined not to let old flames or potential rivalries cast a shadow over the holiday cheer.

# ELEVEN

## *BLAZE*

FINDING ANDREA LOCKE HERE WAS LIKE stumbling across a chapter from my past I'd forgotten I'd bookmarked. She was this bright presence in high school - cheerleader, popular, yet never unkind. My nerdy teenage self had a major thing for her, a crush that felt as intense as anything could at that age. But we'd never been together, and she'd always been with someone else.

Now, here she was, stepping into the McCrae Christmas gathering, a blast from the past in the middle of my present. As I approached her, almost magnetically drawn, she turned, her face lighting up with recognition. "Blaze!" Her greeting was warm, her hug that familiar, slightly distant gesture of old acquaintances reconnecting.

"Andrea," I replied, patting her back before glancing at Aunt Theresa, seeking some clue as to why Andrea was here.

"Andrea moved back to town last year," my aunt explained. "But her mom's away on a cruise over the holidays, and it didn't seem right that Andrea would be all alone when we always have room for one more."

I remembered hearing about Andrea's move to Sacramento after graduation and that she'd gotten married, but I didn't see a ring on Andrea's hand. She must have caught my quick glance down or read the question on my face.

"My husband and I divorced right before Christmas last year."

"Oh, I'm sorry to hear that." I stuck my hands in my pockets, waiting for something else to say. "I'll bet your mom's glad you're home. I'm sure she missed you."

"She did," Andrea agreed, but her smile didn't quite reach her eyes. "And we enjoyed last Christmas together. This year, though ... well, my mom started dating this guy a few months ago, and he surprised her with a cruise for the two of them."

"Andrea happened to be at the dentist's office the same day I went in," Theresa said. "We got to talking, and when she mentioned her mom leaving two days before Christmas, I invited her to join us today."

"And I really appreciate it, Mrs. McCrae."

"Theresa," my aunt said with a smile. "Please."

Then Paris nudged me, her expression urgent, and I realized Trisha was watching us from across the room. Damn. I hadn't considered how this might look to her, how she might misinterpret this blast from my past.

I wanted to explain to her, but then Uncle Patrick's voice boomed through the house, announcing it was time for the feast. With the house full to the brim—kids, partners, and friends—I knew this meal would be a balancing act of family dynamics and unspoken tensions.

Navigating the crowded dining room was like trying to find your seat at a packed Taylor Swift concert. It was a dance of jostling elbows and shuffled steps, a blend of laughter and holiday chatter. Somehow, in this festive shuffle, I ended up next to Andrea in the food line, while Trisha was several people behind, lost in a sea of relatives and friends.

I had this urge to slide back, be near Trisha, and assure her with a look or a small gesture that she wasn't forgotten. But just as I was about to maneuver through the crowd, Andrea's touch on my arm anchored me back to the spot.

"I was hoping you'd be here," she said, her tone

carrying a hint of something I couldn't quite place. "I heard about your position in Baltimore. Johns Hopkins, right? Professor?"

"That's right," I replied, trying to keep the conversation light, "Professor of Education." I should've felt flattered that she had somehow kept up with my career. But my mind was elsewhere, trailing back to Trisha, wondering if she was alright; if she felt out of place.

I saw Rome and Paris not far from her. They were good company, but Rome's friendliness always bordered on flirting. The thought irked me more than I expected.

Andrea bumped against me playfully, pulling me from my thoughts. "You were always so smart," she mused. "It's no surprise you went down the academic path."

I managed a half-hearted "Thanks," my attention divided. A quick glance upfront revealed Aunt Theresa watching us, a knowing smile on her face. She must have had a hand in this, probably thinking it was a pleasant surprise, not knowing about the silent storm brewing inside me.

Obviously, my aunt had no idea I would bring Trisha when she invited Andrea, and besides, I'd made it clear to everybody that Trisha and I weren't a thing, which was probably why my aunt hadn't given me a

# MISTLETOE DETOUR

heads-up about Andrea. She must've thought setting us up would be harmless, maybe even helpful.

Andrea's voice brought me back, asking about my teaching career. "I don't think I could ever be a teacher," she admitted. "I just don't have the patience for it."

I stifled a sigh, resigned to making polite conversation. This was the least I could do for someone who'd had a tough year. "What about you? What's your story these days?"

As she spoke, detailing her plans for a new apartment, I found myself only half-listening. I was stealing glances at Trisha, strategizing how to slip back to her side. I knew the clock was ticking; her dad would text soon, the storm would clear, and then she'd be gone. My time with Trisha was slipping away like sand through my fingers, and I was stuck here, tangled in polite small talk with my high school crush.

I was so fucked!

# TWELVE

## *TRISHA*

Was there such a thing as a twentieth wheel?

I definitely wasn't a third wheel with this many people, but twentieth? That was a distinct possibility.

In this bustling, lively gathering, I felt like an extra in a family movie where everyone else had a defined role. Sure, they were all incredibly welcoming, everyone going out of their way to include me, but still, I couldn't shake the feeling of being an outsider.

Though unrelated by blood, Andrea still had her slice of history with this family. I, on the other hand, was the only real outsider. As the morning progressed, this realization pressed down on me, leaving me feeling claustrophobic in the midst of their warmth and camaraderie.

With the kids eagerly taking their Christmas gifts apart, I took advantage of the opportunity to slip outside for some fresh air and space. The sun, finally breaking through the clouds, was a welcome sight. I tilted my face upwards, soaking in its gentle warmth. The crisp air, a stark contrast to the snowy, frigid weather I'd left behind on the East Coast, felt refreshing, almost liberating.

I meandered down the McCraes' long, winding driveway, relishing the quiet and the chance to stretch my legs. I mused over my childhood fantasies of having siblings, a large family like this. The love, the unbreakable bonds I'd witnessed today brought those old yearnings to the surface. But I hadn't factored in the sheer volume, the overwhelming energy of so many people under one roof.

It was a memorable Christmas with Blaze's family, but it also stirred a pang of homesickness in me. The quiet, more subdued holidays I was used to with my dad suddenly seemed worlds away.

Reaching the end of the driveway, I paused, gazing towards the town. My phone felt heavy in my pocket, a reminder. I pulled it out and dialed my dad's number, needing to hear his voice, to connect with my own slice of family, however small it might be. As the phone rang, I waited, anticipation and a tinge of melancholy mingling within me.

"Hi, Dad," I greeted, my voice lighter despite the whirlwind of emotions inside. "Merry Christmas."

His concern was clear even through the phone. "Everything okay? I was about to text you that the storm has cleared."

I looked down the quiet street, feeling both relieved and hesitant. "That's great. I'll head out soon. I just need to say my goodbyes."

He sensed something in my tone. "You sound like you've had a good time. If you want to stay longer, you can. Remember, we can always have our celebration whenever. We've always been good at that."

It was true. Our little family of two had never been bound by dates on a calendar. Our moments together, whenever they happened, were our celebrations. "Dad, this place is like a festival. Blaze said his family was big, but seeing it is another story."

His next question was more probing. "So, do you think you'll see this Blaze fellow again after this?"

The question hung heavy in the air. "No, I don't think so, Dad." My voice was a whisper, carrying a twinge of regret.

"You could, you know," he encouraged gently. "Perhaps you should finally let someone in?"

"It's not that simple, Dad." I sighed, my thoughts swirling. "And with work, I just don't have time for—"

He interrupted, his tone laced with wisdom. "Trisha, remember to live a little, okay? Don't bury yourself in work."

I almost told him then about the job, the move, the whole upheaval waiting in the wings. But, knowing that sharing that news might cause a storm, I held back. Instead, I steered the conversation toward him. "You're taking it easy, right? Keeping up with Dr. Siegler's advice?"

"Of course," he chuckled. "I'm sticking to the plan."

Our talk shifted to holiday preparations. I felt a twinge of guilt for not having been there to help with the tree, the decorations. But he assured me he'd managed, pacing himself.

"You shouldn't have had to do it alone," I said, my voice tinged with regret.

"Trisha, it's okay. You couldn't control the weather. And it sounds like you needed this break, this... adventure."

His voice had a knowing tone, and I realized he understood more than I gave him credit for. I'd enjoyed my time here, with Blaze, with his family. It was a different world, one I'd only ever imagined.

"I love our family, Dad," I said firmly, wanting him to know that our small duo was more than enough.

He laughed, the sound warming my heart.

I thought of Blaze then, how, in all the chaos, being with him felt like a calm in the storm. But I couldn't dwell on that now. Not when I was about to leave.

"Soon, it'll be just us again," Dad said, a note of anticipation in his voice.

"Can't wait, Dad," I replied, a smile in my voice. "I'm heading back in a minute. I'll text you before I leave."

"Drive safe when you do. And Trisha?"

"Yeah?"

"Merry Christmas, sweetheart."

"Merry Christmas, Dad." I hung up, feeling a blend of emotions. Homesickness, a sense of loss, and a surprising depth of affection for the people I was about to leave behind.

# THIRTEEN

## *BLAZE*

"I have a question that I'm dying to know the answer to," Andrea said, her curiosity clear.

I stifled a sigh. I'd tried to find a polite way to escape Andrea's company and rejoin Trisha, but each attempt had been thwarted.

"As a professor, do you have a lot of students who take your classes because of..." She hesitated, a blush coloring her cheeks, "You know, because you're hot?"

Her forwardness left me speechless.

Dealing with Andrea was challenging. Had she been overly aggressive or outright rude, I would've felt justified in shutting it down immediately, making it clear that I wasn't interested. But she wasn't like that;

she was the same friendly, outgoing person I had been crushing on throughout high school.

In truth, if Trisha hadn't come into the picture, I might have played along with Andrea, maybe even indulged in a bit of harmless flirtation for old times' sake. But Trisha changed everything. Despite the undefined nature of our relationship, and even though we had no plans to continue whatever this was after she left, I couldn't, in good conscience, engage with Andrea on anything beyond a basic, courteous level. What I shared with Trisha, however fleeting, deserved that respect.

"Well, I've had a few students make inappropriate comments, but most are serious about their studies," I replied diplomatically. "My classes are graduate-level, so students are generally more focused on their careers than socializing."

"And Johns Hopkins isn't really a party school, is it?" she prodded, trying to keep the conversation going.

"No, it's not," I said. "That's one reason I wanted to go there in the first place."

"That's right," Andrea said. "You were such a dedicated student, always hitting the books."

I pondered her comment as I reflected on my journey to this point. She had painted a picture of me as always being a serious, dedicated student, but that wasn't the whole truth. After my siblings and I moved in with Theresa and Patrick, my life had been anything but focused. I coasted through my early high school years, doing just enough to get by. I wasn't a troublemaker, but I was definitely lost, struggling to find my place in this new chapter of our lives.

There was also the responsibility I felt for Fury and Rose. I had taken it upon myself to look out for them, even though Theresa and Patrick were more than capable. It took me a while to understand that they didn't need me to shoulder that burden, but that realization didn't lessen my protective instincts toward them.

Everything shifted at the end of my freshman year. An essay I wrote caught the attention of Mr. Shirley, my English teacher. His encouragement was a turning point for me. He saw potential in me that I hadn't seen in myself and urged me to pursue it. That was when I started to apply myself, discovering a passion for learning and a desire to inspire others.

This passion eventually led me towards a career in education.

"So, when does the new semester start?" Andrea asked, bringing me back to the conversation.

"Soon," I said, "I'm flying home in a few days. I had hoped to arrive earlier, but my flight was canceled."

"Your aunt said you and your friend drove here from Chicago?"

"Yes," I replied as I scanned the room for Trisha. A sense of urgency took over when I realized she wasn't there.

"That's a long drive. It's good you had someone to share it with. Did you two plan to fly out together, or was it a coincidence?" Andrea asked, her tone casual.

"We met in the rental car line," I answered absently, my concern for Trisha growing. "I don't even know where she's from," I added, still trying to spot her.

"Really? So you're not dating her?" Andrea seized the opportunity. "You know, maybe we could get together before you leave? Just the two of us?"

I'd already tuned her out. "Excuse me," I said, standing abruptly.

I left Andrea without further explanation, feeling rude but driven by a stronger need to find Trisha. I couldn't shake the feeling that I had somehow let her down. I should have shown her how much she meant to me. Now, it was maybe too late.

Uncle Patrick was the only one in the kitchen. "Hey, have you seen Trisha?" I asked, trying to sound casual.

"She stepped outside for a walk," he told me, his eyes hinting he understood.

A wave of panic surged through me as I realized the situation. Had I inadvertently given Trisha the impression that she was less important to me? There I was, stuck in a conversation with Andrea, my high school crush, while Trisha knew nobody. No wonder she might have felt the need to slip away.

I needed to find her and apologize. I couldn't let her leave, thinking I was some inconsiderate asshole.

Even though I apparently was exactly that.

"Did you see which way she went?"

"Out the front door and down the driveway. You should be able to see which way she turned if you hurry."

I hurried outside, my heart pounding, but I kept my composure, not wanting to cause any alarm. Once out of sight, I hastened my steps, driven by the need to catch up with Trisha. As I reached the end of the driveway, I saw her figure in the distance, moving towards downtown. My walk turned into a jog, my concern growing with each stride.

As I drew closer, I slowed down, mindful not to startle her. Trisha was deep in conversation on her phone. I paused, catching my breath, waiting for her to finish. She finally put her phone away and turned, her expression a mix of surprise and curiosity as she saw me.

Before she could voice her questions, I spoke up, my voice laced with concern. "Are you okay?"

## FOURTEEN

*TRISHA*

"Yes, I'm fine," I replied, trying to mask the tumult of emotions his presence stirred within me. "Just needed a bit of fresh air, that's all."

Blaze relaxed slightly, but his gaze remained fixed on me as if trying to read between the lines. "My uncle saw you slip out. The crowd can be a bit much, huh?"

"You could say that," I chuckled, finding comfort in his understanding. "It's like stepping into a whirlwind in there."

He smiled, a playful glint in his eyes. "I guess we tend to sweep people off their feet – figuratively and literally."

"I'd say you're more of a tornado than a whirlwind," I teased back, feeling the ease of our banter chase away the heaviness of the impending goodbye.

Blaze's smile didn't fade as he stepped a little closer. "Well, I guess there are worse things to be. But hey, if you need a break from the family tornado, I'm here."

I nodded, feeling some relief wash over me. His genuine and earnest concern made it seem a little less overwhelming. "Deal. And thanks, Blaze. It's nice to know I've got an ally in the eye of the storm."

His gaze lingered on me, soft yet intense. "I forget how loud and chaotic my family can be. And distracting. I'm sorry."

I hesitated, unsure how much to reveal. "No, it's all good. I'm just realizing how different this is from what I'm used to."

He stepped closer, his presence both comforting and unsettling. "Different can be good, you know."

"I know," I murmured, our eyes locked in a moment of silent understanding.

Blaze's voice softened. "I wish you didn't have to leave so soon."

The vulnerability in his tone tugged at my heart. "Yeah, me too. But my dad's waiting, and the storm has cleared, so I should probably get going."

Blaze's expression held a hint of disappointment, but he nodded in understanding. "I know, family comes first. But hey, the roads aren't going anywhere. You sure you can't stay just a bit longer?"

I bit my lip, torn between the pull of seeing dad and the desire to linger with Blaze. "It's tempting, really tempting, but I should head out. I've already pushed it by staying all morning."

"Can I at least walk you back? Help with your things?" he asked, his hand outstretched towards me, an unspoken invitation for a few more moments together.

I hesitated...then, giving in to the pull of his presence, I placed my hand in his. His touch was warm, a gentle anchor in my flurry of emotions. "That would be nice, thank you."

Our walk back was a quiet journey filled with shared looks and unspoken thoughts rather than words. It was comfortable, yet it stirred within me a sense of longing, a desire for more moments like these that Blaze so effortlessly brought to life.

As we approached the house, Blaze stopped and faced me, a seriousness in his eyes. "Trisha, I don't know what comes next, but these past few days, they've been..."

"Special," I said, finding the word for both of us. It hung in the air, a perfect descriptor for the whirlwind of emotions and experiences we'd shared.

"Yeah, special," he echoed, and I saw in his eyes a

reflection of the bittersweet mix of feelings churning inside me.

We stood there, caught in a moment that was both an ending and a possibility. Then, with a heavy sigh, I stepped back, breaking the spell. "I should go and say goodbye."

Just then, Blaze surprised me. "There's a little shop nearby, open on Christmas. It's for people who don't have family around or just need a break. They serve great hot chocolate and cookies." He looked almost nervous suggesting it, an unexpectedly charming side of him.

A smile tugged at my lips. Maybe I could stretch this goodbye a little longer. After all, even my dad had hinted at staying a bit more. "I think I'd like that, though it's kind of funny to think about drinking hot chocolate when it's this warm out."

Blaze grinned. "I know what you mean. It took a while, but I'm more used to the colder winters now. My first winter driving in the snow, I hit a patch of black ice and nearly wrecked my car."

His laugh, light and infectious, drew a genuine chuckle from me. "I guess black ice is something of a rite of passage," I said, my tone playful. "But I'm glad you were okay."

Blaze shrugged, a hint of a smile still playing on his

lips. "It was definitely a wake-up call. Gave me a new respect for winter driving."

As we strolled towards the cozy shop, our steps fell into a comfortable rhythm. Blaze's anecdote about black ice had painted a picture of his life, likely somewhere on the frosty East Coast. My curiosity about the life I knew nothing of, bubbled inside me. I remembered the little tidbit London had said about his high school days jamming to the Backstreet Boys, and it made me smile.

But I resisted the urge to pepper him with questions. We had established rules, unspoken lines we agreed not to cross, to keep things simple, uncomplicated. And as much as I wanted to delve deeper, to understand the man beside me, I knew this wasn't the time. This walk, these moments, they were precious—a fleeting connection in our otherwise separate lives. I didn't want to taint them with a barrage of queries and the inevitable "what-ifs" that would follow.

Yet, as Blaze's hand wrapped around mine, a surge of warmth washed over me, pushing aside any lingering hesitation. His touch was electric, sparking a connection that felt both thrilling and right. His fingers laced with mine, a silent promise in the simple gesture.

I looked up at him, finding his gaze already on me. It was deep and searching, as if he was trying to read my thoughts, to understand the emotions swirling within me. In his eyes, I saw a reflection of my own feelings - a mixture of longing, curiosity, and a hint of something more, something deeper.

Our encounter had been sudden, passionate, and completely unforgettable. Somewhere inside me, I knew I would hold onto these memories and emotions for years to come. Blaze wasn't just some passing fling anymore; he had become a permanent fixture in my life story, one that I would return to again and again during quiet times alone or when lost in thought.

"Tell me more about this shop," I said, needing something else to focus on besides our physical connection.

"Well, it's been open as long as I can remember," Blaze said. "The couple who owns it, Ma and Pa Ulrich, have been old as long as I can remember. They're like grandparents for everyone in the area. Go all out for every holiday with decorations, and they're always open on holidays."

"That's really sweet," I said.

I didn't need Blaze to point out the shop to me because I could spot it as soon as we rounded a corner. Besides being the only open place on the street, it was covered with decorations. Garlands with glittery red balls strung across the edge of the roof. Multi-colored lights around the big glass window and the door.

Wreaths on both. I even saw a Christmas tree through the window before we went inside.

The moment we stepped through the threshold, a warm wave of cinnamon and spice flooded my senses, mingling with the strains of Christmas carols that swirled through the air, wrapping the cozy space in an embrace of festive cheer. The intimate dining area, with its smattering of patrons, seemed to pause, their attention momentarily drawn to us as a chorus of bells chimed above the door and announced our entrance. Brimming with jovial energy, a robust voice boomed from the counter, "Merry Christmas!"

"Merry Christmas," Blaze said in return as he led the way to the counter. "Can we get two hot chocolates and a box of a dozen mixed cookies?"

"You're one of the McCraes, aren't you?" The frail-looking woman behind the counter said as she slid a box over to him.

"Yes, ma'am," he said, not bothering to correct her on his last name.

That must've been weird, I realized suddenly. For the Carideos, it might've been a little strange, but their mom had taken the McCrae name, and having a stepfamily was fairly normal. The three Gracens, however, must've had difficulty explaining who they were and how they fit into the family dynamic.

"Here." She set another box on the counter. "This

one is on the house. You tell your dad it's a thank you for helping us decorate."

After paying for our hot chocolate and cookies, Blaze motioned for me to go to a corner booth where we could have our drinks. When we sat down, I reached out and put my hand on his, giving it a squeeze before I turned my attention to my drink.

"Who were you talking to before?" Blaze asked. When I gave him a confused look, he clarified. "You were on the phone earlier. Your dad?"

"Yeah, I wanted to wish him a Merry Christmas and find out if the weather there had finally cleared." I thought I saw a shadow cross his face, but it was gone before I could really analyze it.

I sipped the hot chocolate, its sweetness a sharp contrast to the bittersweet tang of knowing our time together was drawing to a close. Blaze watched me over the rim of his cup, his eyes a study in hidden depths.

"Kind of ironic, isn't it?" he said with a smile. "Here we are in San Ramon, enjoying hot chocolate in a café that's toasty enough to be a beach in summer while the rest of the country is buried under snow."

I laughed, appreciating his light-heartedness. "It's like we're in a tropical bubble while the rest of the world is in a snow globe," I replied, joining in the playful banter.

He grinned, setting his cup down. "That's the perfect way to put it."

Leaning back, Blaze's gaze lingered on me, and I felt a familiar flutter in my stomach—not from the warmth of the café but from the connection that seemed to crackle between us.

We stayed in the café longer than necessary, reluctant to face the goodbye that awaited us. Each laugh and glance we shared was bittersweet, a reminder that our time in this warm, sunlit haven was drawing to a close.

Neither of us spoke as we made to leave, but just as we reached the door, someone called out behind us.

"You have to kiss!"

We stopped, both of us confused, as we looked back to find a middle-aged woman with purple hair grinning at us.

"What?" I asked.

She pointed. "Mistletoe. Kiss already."

Blaze and I looked up to see mistletoe hanging above the door.

"Kiss her, buddy. Or I will," a man bellowed from one table.

Everyone laughed, but there wasn't even a hint of malice in the sound. In fact, I was laughing along with them.

At least, I was until Blaze's mouth covered mine. It

was a slow, sweet kiss, made all the sweeter by the taste of chocolate and nutmeg from our treats. Slow, but not deep, still appropriate for our public surroundings.

However, the thoughts going through my head were definitely *not* public-friendly. Thoughts about wrapping my legs around his waist and asking him to take me against a wall. Thoughts of dragging him to the closest hotel and locking us inside a room so we could fuck until we rang in the new year.

Shit.

I took a step back, well aware of how flushed my face was and how ragged my breathing had become despite the relative innocence of the kiss.

His eyes met mine, and I saw all the heat and the desire I felt reflected at me.

"Let's head back to the house," he breathed. "Can you stay for an hour longer? One hour more with my family?"

I knew what he was really asking. An hour longer with him.

# FIFTEEN

## *BLAZE*

My entire body still buzzing from the kiss, Trisha and I approached the house. We walked in silence, a content heaviness hanging between us.

Trisha hadn't pulled away when I took her hand, a gesture I held onto as a sign she didn't regret our kiss. However, Trisha was leaving soon, and I wasn't ready to face that finality. Of course, I could find her again if I wanted, but I respected her enough to let her go if that's what she wished.

As we reached the doorstep, a realization hit me like a sudden gust of wind, clear and undeniable. I absolutely did not want this to be the end. The thought of never seeing her again, not exploring what we had started, felt like a missed opportunity I would regret. It was a shift in my mindset I hadn't expected, a desire for something more than a fleeting holiday romance.

I wanted things to change. I wanted to see her again.

I wanted more than this.

Well, damn.

I hadn't seen that coming.

Inside, Trisha's cheeks were flushed from the cold, her smile brighter than the string of lights tangled in the fir branches. The room hummed with holiday cheer, but I caught a few raised eyebrows, and my siblings exchanged sly looks. No one questioned our brief escape as everyone settled into playing holiday games, calling for us to join them.

Trisha's grin stretched wide, announcing she had another hour to spare. I felt a knot form in my stomach when Aunt Theresa nudged Andrea and me together for the game. This matchmaking charade was wearing thin. Even though Aunt Theresa's heart was in the right place, her attempts to rekindle things with my former crush fell flat. Catching Trisha's gaze, I managed a wry half-smile, trying to telegraph my irritation with the setup. She flashed back a grin that seemed to read my thoughts, sending a pleasant heat through me.

Of course, Rome quickly jumped at the chance to partner with Trisha. I gritted my teeth as he turned on the charm, his flirtatious banter eliciting giggles from her. I knew it was innocent, but the possessive side of me bristled. I had to resist the urge to stride over and stake my claim.

When Trisha casually placed her hand on Rome's arm, laughter in her eyes, I had to look away. I busied myself fiddling with the game pieces, trying to ignore the irrational flare of jealousy. She wasn't mine. I had no right to be upset. But the want simmering beneath the surface made it difficult to stay rational.

The game unfolded before me, but my attention wandered as if I were a viewer lost in the wrong scene of a familiar play.

"I'm grabbing something to drink," I said suddenly, getting to my feet.

I needed a moment, just a minute, to gather my thoughts.

The kitchen was empty and quiet except for the refrigerator's gentle hum and the soft glow from the overhead light. I grabbed a glass, filled it with water, and took a long drink, hoping it would quench more than just my physical thirst. The water did little to soothe the knot in my stomach, though.

"Don't overthink this," I muttered, leaning against the counter. "It was never meant to be." I had no right to feel sad, jealous, or possessive. Trisha and I had an understanding—no strings attached, no messy emotions. It was always meant to be fleeting.

I set the glass down with more force than necessary and ran a hand through my hair. My reflection in the windowpane showed a man wrestling with his own rules.

The kitchen door swung open, and Andrea strolled in, her steps silent on the tile floor. Her eyes locked onto mine with an intensity that had been absent before. "There you are," she said with a coy smile. "You missed our turn."

"Sorry, but I was just—"

Before I could finish, Andrea stepped closer, her hand reaching up to touch my arm. Her fingers felt like fire against my skin. She inched closer, backing me into a corner where a sprig of mistletoe dangled innocently above us.

"Oh, look," she whispered, her lips curving into a playful smirk. "Mistletoe."

And then she kissed me.

It wasn't gentle or hesitant; it was demanding, insistent—a stark contrast to the kiss I'd shared with Trisha less than an hour earlier. My mind reeled as I placed my hands on Andrea's shoulders and gently but firmly pushed her away.

"Andrea," I began, my voice strained.

The kitchen door creaked open again, and there

stood Trisha, her eyes catching mine for a split second before they flicked to Andrea's flushed face and then back to me.

I watched as Trisha's features shifted like sand beneath a changing tide until they settled into an expression so neutral it felt like a slap.

"I think it's time for me to head out," Trisha said evenly, her voice betraying none of the warmth I'd come to cherish over our journey together.

The air seemed to thicken around me as I stood there, trapped between Andrea's lingering presence and Trisha's impending departure.

"Trisha," I started, but she turned on her heel without another word, leaving me grasping at silence.

That's it. Game over.

"Go after her."

Andrea's unexpected encouragement jolted me back to reality.

I blinked, surprised. "What?"

Her smile was genuine, devoid of any prior coquettishness. "I see it, Blaze. There's something real between you and her. She's who you want."

Struggling to find words, I stammered, "Andrea, I..."

"You're a good guy," she continued, her voice warm yet firm. "I liked that, especially after my last fucked up relationship. But I won't be a second choice or a consolation prize." A touch of sadness flickered in her eyes. "If you really care about Trisha, go tell her. And, please apologize to her from me. I wouldn't have kissed you if I'd known."

Her understanding took me aback. "Thank you," I managed. "And I'm sorry about Aunt Theresa's matchmaking efforts. She was just trying to help."

Andrea nodded. "I get it. And remember, you deserve someone who chooses you first, too."

I leaned in and hugged her in a friendly gesture. "Your ex was a fucking idiot to let you go."

She smiled, a soft chuckle escaping her. "Now, go get your girl."

Wasting no time, I bolted out the kitchen door, bypassing the living room to avoid any family interference. The realization that I might lose Trisha was a weight pressing down on me, driving me forward.

I rounded the house, my heart sinking as I saw Trisha's car already making its way down the driveway.

I weighed my options. Hiring a private investigator to track her down felt too invasive, too impersonal. Not to mention it would make me look like a psycho stalker. Forgetting about her was out of the question. That left me with one choice—to follow her.

Without a second thought, I grabbed the keys to the family's spare car and tore after her. It didn't take me long to catch up. I kept a safe distance, mindful not to make her uncomfortable or put her at risk. It was only an hour's drive to San Francisco, after all. The thought of what to say and how to express how I felt raced through my head.

The remnants of the storm were evident as we exited the highway. Downed branches and debris littered the roadside, a stark reminder of the hazards Trisha could have faced if she'd left earlier.

The drive became a test of nerves, my hands white-knuckled on the steering wheel as I focused on Trisha's car ahead. Following someone without a clear destination in mind was harder than I'd imagined.

Pulling into the parking lot next to an apartment building, my heart raced. If I didn't catch her now, I might lose my chance entirely. I found a spot and rushed out, only to see Trisha waiting by her car. Her expression was unreadable, but the fact that she waited for me was enough to keep my hope alive.

"I didn't kiss her," I said quickly, the words tumbling out. I ran a hand through my hair, frustrated at my own lack of finesse. "She kissed me, but it wasn't what I wanted. I was caught off guard, that's all."

Trisha's lips twitched slightly, a hint of amusement in her eyes that spurred me on.

"Andrea was someone I desired in high school, but that's all in the past now," I continued, trying to lighten the mood. "Back then, I also thought wearing Axe body spray was the peak of sophistication."

Her laughter broke through, easing the tension just a bit.

"Let me be clear, Trisha," I said earnestly. "My feelings for Andrea are long gone. You're the one I'm crazy about and can't get out of my mind."

Trisha's eyes glistened, a mix of emotions playing across her face. I took a deep breath, gathering my thoughts.

"Trisha, what we've shared these past days... it's been more than just a casual fling for me," I confessed. "I've come to care about you more than I've allowed myself to feel for anyone in a very long time. It's been incredible, and I don't want it to end here. I know we have a lot to figure out, but I want to give us a real shot to see where this could go."

I stepped closer, stopping just short of reaching out to her. I wanted to touch her, to pull her close, but I held back, waiting for her response.

"If you don't feel the same, if you want to leave things as they are, I'll understand," I said, my voice steady despite the turmoil inside. "I'll respect whatever decision you make."

Silence stretched between us, a defining moment that held the potential to change everything. I waited, my heart in my throat, hoping she felt the same way.

# SIXTEEN

## *TRISHA*

The realization that Blaze had followed me, leaving his family behind on Christmas Day to find me, was both startling and touching. His presence in the parking lot of my dad's building was unexpected. Despite the whirlwind of emotions inside me, I needed to hear him out. I couldn't ignore his determination.

As Blaze poured out his feelings, confessing his desire for more than just a fleeting connection, I found myself hanging on every word. It wasn't just the surprise of his confession that held me captive; it was the earnest hope in his eyes, a reflection of the hope that had been quietly growing in my heart.

When he finished, the silence between us was thick with anticipation. He didn't move closer, respecting the space between us, giving me time to process, to respond.

The words tumbled out of me almost of their own accord. "I feel the same way," I admitted, my voice thick with emotion. "I don't want this to end either."

Our bodies collided, one moment separate, the next entwined. I couldn't say whose movement started our contact - it seemed instinctive, inevitable. We stood there, my breath catching as his hands wove themselves into my hair. Then his lips met mine, a sensuous pressure that sent shivers down my spine.

His kiss deepened, his tongue tracing along my lower lip before slipping inside my mouth. My response was immediate, hungry even, my tongue meeting his halfway. The taste of him was exhilarating, a heady mix of coffee and something uniquely Blaze.

My arms snaked around his neck, pulling him impossibly closer until our bodies aligned perfectly against each other. Any remaining distance between us disappeared, leaving no room for air, only heat. It felt natural, as if we had always belonged together like this. And maybe we did. Maybe we always would.

I'd completely forgotten that we were standing in a parking lot, in full view of anyone who happened to be around, until someone cleared their throat.

Dad.

Shit.

MISTLETOE DETOUR

Flustered and caught in an unexpected lip lock with Blaze, I felt a mix of mortification and merriment under my dad's eagle eye. "Merry Christmas, Dad," I squeezed out, trying to keep my composure.

Blaze's response to my father's appearance was practically comical, a cocktail of shock and unease. "Oh, um, hello, er, Mr. Easton," he fumbled. His cheeks turned a delightful shade of crimson, which made me want to giggle, but I somehow restrained myself.

Dad, ever the easygoing type, extended a handshake. "Call me Matthew. You must be the young man who braved the Chicago drive with my daughter."

"Yes, sir. Blaze Gracen," Blaze replied, his handshake firm despite the earlier fluster.

Dad's warmth and casual demeanor seemed to put Blaze a bit more at ease. "Why don't you come inside?" he offered.

Blaze hesitated, not wanting to intrude, but Dad insisted. "It's no intrusion. We'd be glad to have you."

The familiarity of my dad's apartment building washed over me as we approached the entrance. I'd called this place home for years before moving to New York. The big city never felt quite like home to me, but maybe Baltimore will feel more like it than the bustling streets of Manhattan.

We reached my dad's door, and as we walked

inside, the jumble of thoughts about my new job and relocation plans buzzed at the edge of my consciousness. I wanted to tell Dad my big plans for us, but now wasn't the time. We'd lost enough days to the holiday chaos, and now Blaze had become an unexpected addition to our reunion.

I excused myself to head to my old bedroom. It was strange to see it transformed into a guest room, its walls stripped of posters and shelves cleared of childhood knick-knacks.

Dropping my bag on the small bed, I paused for a moment. The space felt so different now—but not entirely foreign. My eyes flickered to Blaze, who stood at the threshold, looking slightly out of place amid the frills and lace that still adorned some corners of the room.

A rogue thought flitted through my mind—Blaze sharing this bed with me—sparking a fluttering in my stomach. It was a tantalizing notion, anticipation mixed with excitement at what might happen if we gave in to our desires in this small sanctuary from my past.

Shaking off those thoughts as quickly as they came, I turned to him with a determined smile.

"Let's go hang out with Dad," I said.

Rejoining Dad in the living room, I hovered in the doorway, leaning against the frame as Dad launched into a story from my childhood.

"...and there was Trisha, not even five years old, reading the newspaper cover to cover. I knew then she was destined for great things," Dad finished, beaming with pride.

Blaze grinned back at him. "I can certainly see that. She's got quite the sharp mind."

I rolled my eyes playfully. "Don't let him fool you. I wasn't reading the newspaper back then. Just looking at the pictures."

Dad chuckled. "Maybe so, but you picked up reading faster than any other kid I knew." He turned to Blaze. "You'll have to stay for dinner. I want to hear all about this cross-country adventure you two had."

Blaze hesitated. "Oh, I wouldn't want to impose..."

But Dad brushed aside his objection with a wave of his hand. "Nonsense. It's no trouble at all."

I added my own insistence until Blaze relented with a smile. "Well, alright then. Dinner it is."

In the kitchen, Blaze and I worked side by side with Dad to get the food on the table. It all felt so natural, so easy, the three of us orbiting around each other in effortless choreography. As I set down the salad bowl, I noticed Dad lean in close to Blaze, whispering something that made Blaze duck his head with an embarrassed little laugh. But when Dad clapped him on the shoulder approvingly, Blaze's face lit up.

Watching their exchange, something warm and

hopeful bloomed in my chest. Dad's obvious delight in Blaze's company told me everything I needed to know. His blessing meant the world to me, even if Blaze and I still navigated our feelings. Just knowing Dad approved lifted a weight I hadn't realized I was carrying.

As we settled around the table, the buzz of contentment remained. Dad filled my glass with wine, his eyes crinkling at the corners as he smiled at me. "To new adventures," he toasted.

I smiled back, raising my glass. "To new adventures." *And to the one sitting right beside me*, I added silently.

As we dug into the food, Blaze turned the conversation to Dad's love of classic car restoration. "What's your dream car to work on?" he asked. Dad's face lit up at the question. He launched into an animated description of his vision for rebuilding a '67 Chevy Impala. I leaned back, content to listen as their discussion flowed. Blaze's questions showed genuine interest in my dad's passion. He even offered suggestions on how to track down rare parts, making Dad's eyes gleam with appreciation.

The evening passed in a warm haze of good food and easy conversation. But a somber mood crept in as the dishes were cleared and leftovers packed away. Blaze stood, stretching, and announced regretfully that it was time he headed out.

I followed him down to the parking lot, the chill of the night air doing nothing to dampen the heat that had built between us over dinner. As he turned to face me beside his car, neither of us spoke at first. Then, in a rush of movement, his hands were in my hair, his lips finding mine hungrily. I melted into him, savoring the feel of his body pressed to mine, his fingers tangled in my curls. We came up for air, both breathing hard, foreheads touching.

"I don't want this to be over," I whispered, voicing the fear that had taken root in my mind. He kissed me again, softer this time.

"It's not over. I'll see you again soon, I promise." His words were reassuring, but uncertainty still gnawed at me as he got into his car. I stepped back, arms wrapped around myself against the cold.

Watching his taillights fade into the distance, I couldn't stop the nagging thought - what if this was the last time I'd ever see him? We'd made no concrete plans and set no date for meeting again. The future stretched before me, vast and unknown. But remembering his hands' touch and the sincerity in his voice when he'd said we'd meet again, I clung to hope. Whatever lay ahead, somehow, our paths would cross once more. I had to believe it with everything in me. Because the alternative–never seeing Blaze again–was one I refused to accept.

## SEVENTEEN

*BLAZE*

I HAD BARELY DRIVEN OUT OF TOWN WHEN I KNEW I was making a mistake. I should be with Trisha, not driving away from her. She was everything I never knew I wanted - funny, sexy, adventurous. Our road trip may have started as a matter of convenience, but it had become so much more.

I turned the car around, eager to go to her, but then hesitated. It was late on Christmas night. She deserved to spend this time with her dad without my sudden reappearance complicating things. I'd give her tonight. First thing tomorrow morning, I'd find her and convince her we should try to make this work.

Resigned to waiting and not wanting the drive back to San Ramon, I headed for the Four Seasons.

The hotel loomed like a beacon as I pulled up, a luxurious sanctuary in the midst of my tumultuous thoughts. Soon after, I found myself in a suite that whispered wealth and comfort, but the plush surroundings did little to soothe my restlessness.

I cracked open the minibar, letting the cool air wash over me. A miniature bottle of whiskey caught my eye—amber liquid promising temporary solace. I poured it into a glass, ice cubes clinking like distant bells.

As I sank into an overstuffed chair, my mind played a relentless tug-of-war. Trisha was out there somewhere on the East Coast; Baltimore was my home base. We'd danced around personal details like two actors avoiding stage directions.

I'd always held that long-distance relationships were like trying to keep a boat afloat with duct tape—eventually, the water wins. But Trisha wasn't just any passing ship; she was more akin to an unsinkable vessel.

Was she worth the shot? The whiskey warmed my throat as decisiveness settled in my bones.

Yes.

First light would find me at her dad's doorstep, laying it all on the line. No half measures or hesitations—I'd ask Trisha Easton to take a leap with me into the unknown because sometimes, just sometimes, you meet someone who makes every mile between you seem trivial.

---

THE MORNING SUN had barely stretched its fingers across the sky when I stood in front of Trisha's dad's apartment door, my hand hovering over the doorbell. The previous night had been a whirlwind of conflicting emotions, but one thing was clear—I couldn't let Trisha walk out of my life without at least trying to keep her in it.

I pressed the bell and waited, shifting from foot to foot. The door swung open, revealing Matthew, his expression a mixture of surprise and warmth.

"Blaze! Didn't expect to see you so soon. Come on in," he said, stepping aside.

"Thanks, but I can't stay. I came for Trisha," I replied, urgency lining my words.

Matthew's face fell slightly. "She left for the airport already, headed back home."

A knot formed in my stomach. "Why'd she leave so sudden? I thought she'd stay at least another day or two?"

He sighed, running a hand through his sandy hair. "We had a bit of a spat last night after you left. She's been on me about moving east with her, thinks it's better for my health."

"And you don't want to go?"

He chuckled ruefully. "I'm not ready to be babysat by my daughter just yet."

I nodded in understanding. "Which airline is she flying with? I need to catch her before she leaves."

Matthew paused, thinking. "Not entirely sure, but she's got a bunch of flying miles with United."

"Thanks," I said, turning on my heel.

"Blaze," Matthew called after me as I strode toward my car.

I glanced back.

"You really care about her," he stated more than asked.

"I do," I admitted, surprised at how easily the truth came out.

"Then go get her," he said with a smile that seemed to say he knew more than he let on.

I didn't need to be told twice. Trisha Easton would not slip through my fingers—not if I had anything to say about it.

I hustled out of Matthew's apartment building, my heart thumping like a drum in my chest. The crisp morning air bit at my cheeks as I jogged to the car. Trisha was out there, probably navigating the chaos of airport security, and here I was, wasting precious seconds. I had to catch her before her flight took off.

As the engine roared to life, I pictured Trisha's electric blue eyes, the way they sparkled when she laughed. The memory fueled my determination. She couldn't leave—not without hearing what I had to say.

Traffic snarled ahead, a sea of brake lights and exhaust. My grip on the steering wheel tightened. Of all days, why did there have to be traffic now? Every minute trapped in this gridlock felt like an eternity slipping through my fingers.

I wove through the lanes, my gaze fixed on openings in the congestion as if they were lifelines. The urgency was a living thing inside me, clawing its way up my throat.

Finally, the airport loomed before me, but victory was short-lived. The parking lot was a labyrinth of cars and pedestrians. I circled like a hawk hunting its prey, desperate for an open spot.

At last, I wedged my car into a space that seemed barely big enough to fit. I slammed the door behind me and bolted toward the terminal. My legs pumped hard against the pavement, each stride an echo of Trisha's name in my head.

Time was the enemy now—a relentless tick-tock in my ears as I dodged travelers and luggage carts. I had to reach her gate before it was too late.

I raced through the terminal, my heart pounding in my chest. I should've asked Matthew where Trisha lived. That one detail would've narrowed down my search, given me a city to aim for. But I hadn't, and now I was sprinting on a hope and a prayer that she'd still be here, somewhere beyond the security gates. All I remembered was she mentioned New York once.

I made a beeline for the United counter, sweat dotting my brow. "One ticket to JFK," I panted to the agent, the closest destination I could think of that made any sense. "When's the next flight?"

She tapped away at her keyboard, eyes flicking up to meet mine. "Leaves in forty-five minutes," she said, sliding a boarding pass across the counter.

As I approached the security line, my heart sank. The queue snaked back and forth like some kind of twisted metal serpent, packed with holiday travelers and their overstuffed carry-ons. I didn't have time for this. Not now.

Taking a deep breath, I approached a security officer standing near the entrance to the line. His badge read "Officer Daniels," and he watched the crowd with sharp eyes.

"Excuse me, Officer Daniels," I began, my voice urgent but steady. "I'm in a bit of a situation here. The woman I—I need to speak with is about to board a flight, and I need to get through security fast."

Officer Daniels looked me over, perhaps seeing the desperation in my eyes or the tension in my posture.

"What's her name?" he asked.

"Trisha Easton," I replied.

He nodded slowly, as if deciding. "Follow me," he said curtly.

With a grateful nod, I fell into step behind him as he led me to an express lane they had for situations like mine. My gratitude toward Officer Daniels couldn't be overstated as we bypassed the winding line of passengers.

Once through security, thanks to Daniels' help, I bolted toward the departure boards—massive screens filled with destinations and flight numbers. My eyes scanned quickly for United flights; there were several departing soon.

The terminal was a living organism—a cacophony of announcements and conversations, children's laughter mingling with the roll of suitcase wheels on tile. My gaze darted from face to face, searching for those distinctive electric blue eyes and chestnut curls that would stand out in any crowd.

There! A flash of blue—no, it was just a scarf wrapped around another traveler's neck. My heart lurched with each false alarm.

The pressure mounted with each passing minute; time was slipping away like sand through my fingers.

She could be boarding right now, heading off into her life without ever knowing how much these last few days had changed me.

I weaved through the crowd, sidestepping a child chasing after a rolling toy car and nearly colliding with a man buried in his phone. Excuse me's and sorry's fell from my lips in an endless stream as I pressed on, relentless in my search for Trisha.

Another glimpse of chestnut curls had me quickening my pace—only to deflate when the woman turned around and her eyes were brown, not the striking blue that haunted my dreams.

The digital clock above gate C14 mocked me as it ticked closer to boarding time for JFK—my arbitrary destination based on Trisha's wake mention. With each passing second, hope dwindled. Had she already passed through one of these gates? Was she already soaring above the clouds while I was stuck on the ground?

My breaths came quick and shallow as panic threatened to take hold. But giving up wasn't an option—I couldn't let it be. Not when so much was left unsaid between us. Not when every fiber of my being screamed that she was worth every effort.

With determined strides, I continued my search through the bustling airport—hoping against hope that fate hadn't taken her from me just yet.

I raced past a blur of shops and faces, each step propelling me forward with a mixture of dread and determination. Then, like a lighthouse cutting through the fog, I saw her—Trisha, standing near a gate that wasn't JFK but Baltimore. My heart stalled and then kicked into overdrive.

"Trisha!" I called out, my voice threading through the hum of airport life. Elbowing past a couple dragging their luggage, I closed the distance between us.

She turned at the sound of her name, her electric blue eyes widening in surprise. "Blaze? What are you doing here?"

The final boarding call crackled over the intercom, igniting urgency in my veins. I reached her just as the attendant began to close the gate.

"Trisha," I said, breathless from both the run and the swell of emotions threatening to choke me. "I had to see you—to tell you..."

Her gaze searched mine, confusion etched on her beautiful face. The air between us crackled with tension and unspoken questions.

"I realized something after I left last night," I continued, my voice steady despite the chaos inside me. "I don't want to say goodbye—not now, not ever."

Her lips parted slightly, but no words came out. She just stood there as if time had stilled around us.

"Stay with me," I pleaded, the weight of everything

we'd shared hanging in the balance. "Let's see where this goes."

The gate agent cleared her throat impatiently, but we were in our own world now—one where only our choices mattered.

# EIGHTEEN

## *TRISHA*

The hustle of the airport blurred into the background as I spotted him, an unexpected anchor in the sea of travelers. Blaze stood there, a touch of disbelief etching his rugged features as our gazes locked. I couldn't help the flutter in my chest, a mixture of surprise and something more potent.

"Trisha," he breathed out, and I heard my name like a melody from his lips.

"Blaze," I returned, feeling a smile spread across my face despite the whirlwind of emotions. The distance between us disappeared in a few strides, and before I knew it, we were wrapped in an embrace that felt like coming home.

"I didn't think I'd see you again," he admitted, pulling back just enough to search my eyes.

"Neither did I," I said, the honesty in my voice mirroring his. "But here you are."

He nodded, a gentle seriousness taking over. "I need to tell you something—something important." His hands rested on my shoulders as if grounding himself. "I haven't stopped thinking about you since last night. You've been... you've changed things for me."

My heart raced with his words, warm and unexpected, like the sun breaking through on a cloudy day.

"Blaze, I—" A tangle of words fought to escape but got caught somewhere between my heart and my throat.

He smiled softly, easing the tension. "It's okay. We don't have to figure everything out right now."

The sincerity in his voice coaxed me back from the edge of panic. Taking a deep breath, I found the courage to share what weighed on me. "My dad's health—it's not good. And with this new job at Johns Hopkins, I'm trying to get him to move closer."

His expression turned to one of surprise. "Did you say Johns Hopkins?"

I nodded, confused.

"You know, I'm actually a professor at Johns Hopkins."

Laughter bubbled up from within me, unbidden and pure. "You're kidding! They just hired me!"

His chuckle joined mine, filling the space between us with an easy joy that felt both fresh and familiar.

"So we'll be colleagues then?" His blue-violet eyes sparkled with amusement.

"It seems fate does have a sense of humor," I quipped back.

We shifted into a more serious conversation as we sat at one of the terminal benches. The surrounding noise faded into a distant hum as I explained my father's situation in more detail—the diagnosis that shadowed our days with its uncertainty and my hopes that the renowned specialists at Johns Hopkins could provide better treatment options for him.

Blaze listened intently, his warm blue-violet eyes never wavering from mine as he absorbed every word with a compassion that I found both comforting and steadying.

"I'll help however I can," he promised earnestly, his voice low but sincere. "Whether talking to the top specialists or being there for emotional support when things get difficult. I'll even help convince your dad to make the move, if that's what it takes for him to get the best possible care."

I nodded, touched by his selfless offer of help. The airport assistant at the boarding desk for my flight was now roping off the entrance, the boarding call echoing over the intercom.

"Trisha?" Blaze asked tentatively when he noticed my lack of movement towards the gate.

"I'm not going," I said softly but with resolve, the words surprising me even as they tumbled from my lips. "Not yet."

His hand reached out again, linking with mine—a simple yet intimate gesture that somehow felt like everything in that fleeting moment.

A mischievous glint animated my expression as I tilted my head to meet his gaze. "Now, about that suite at the Four Seasons you mentioned? I hear it's quite the fancy place, and I still have a present for you."

## *BLAZE*

TRISHA'S CALF-LENGTH coat dropped to the floor before the door, revealing a black lace negligee with a pair of matching black, barely-there panties. The top revealed a generous amount of cleavage, the line just above the darker flesh of her nipples, but the fabric was sheer enough that I could see her nipples pebbling as I stared. She slipped off her shoes and came toward me, putting a little extra sway in her hips. When she was within touching distance, she stopped and tipped her head back so she could meet my eyes.

"Ready to unwrap your present?" Her voice was low, husky, and went straight to my cock.

All thoughts of us finally talking about what came next flew right out of my mind. It was a little difficult to think when the blood was rushing away from my head. Well, to think about anything but the half-naked woman in front of me.

I cleared my throat. "I'm unsure if this means I'm naughty or nice."

"I'm hoping for naughty."

It was those words that sent me to my knees right there. I put my hands on her hips and pressed a kiss to the space just below her belly button. She shivered, goosebumps breaking across her skin. I smiled and began kissing lower. The waistband of her panties. Her hipbones. The top of her mound.

"Spread your legs," I ordered.

She complied immediately, and I traced my tongue along the damp crotch of her panties. She sucked in a breath, her hands going to my shoulders. I pulled aside the fabric, exposing that soft pink flesh. Leaning forward, I licked her, smiling when her hips jerked, pushing her closer to my mouth. Keeping one hand gripping her hip firmly, I worked my tongue between her lips, groaning as the taste of her burst across my tastebuds.

I'd never been the sort of man who disliked giving oral, but with her, it was more than just the basic enjoyment of bringing pleasure to my partner. There was something primal, almost possessive, about having my mouth on this part of her, circling her opening before thrusting my tongue into her core. Teasing her clit with quick flicks and soft little licks until it swelled.

"Blaze, fuck, Blaze…"

Her muscles tensed, her breathing quickened, and I knew she was close. I took her clit between my lips, applying gentle suction as I slid a finger inside her. Her nails dug into my shoulders, biting even through my shirt, and the pain made my cock even harder. Just as she started telling me she was going to come, I pushed a second finger into her and crooked it, running my fingertips down the smooth wall until I found the slightly rough patch that marked her g-spot. Increasing my suction on her clit, I tapped that spot once, twice, and she called out my name.

Her body curled over mine as she came, a sweet release lingering on my lips and tongue. I held her upright, let her cling to me as she shook. Nearly a minute passed before she straightened, her face flushed. I smiled at her as I got to my feet, brushing my lips across hers as I went.

Taking her hand, I led her to the bed and helped her as she climbed on it with legs that were still shaky. Settling back on the pillows, she gave me a sultry look and tugged on the bow, holding her top together. It fell apart easily, exposing those beautiful breasts of hers and leaving her clad only in her panties, which were still pulled to one side.

"Gorgeous," I murmured as I knelt in front of her, my clothes discarded in a pile on the floor.

"Likewise." Her gaze was hungry as it ran over me, stopping at my waist.

I may have been a little smug as I wrapped my hand around the base of my cock and gave it a stroke.

"Condom?" she asked as she hooked her thumbs in the waistband of her panties and slipped them off.

I picked up the condom from my jeans pocket, and as I ripped open the packet, she ran her fingers between her breasts and down over her stomach, inching toward the juncture of her legs. I couldn't look away as she spread her lips, opening herself up to me. My hands shook as I rolled on the condom, my need for her nearly overwhelming. She ran her middle finger across her clit, letting out a moan.

The sound was my undoing.

I dropped over her, propping myself up on one elbow as I took myself in hand, guiding the tip to her opening.

"Yes."

She answered my unasked question, and in the next breath, I was pushing inside. Her muscles rippled around me as I fought my way deeper. She was wet but tight, and by the time I was completely sheathed inside her, we were both panting, a thin sheet of sweat glistening on our skin.

I held myself still, our gazes locked, and I felt myself falling into those blue depths, losing myself in them. It was as if I could feel her body as well as my own, like we were one and the same. When she stirred under me, I moved, grinding against her with every other thrust to put the right amount of friction and pressure on her clit. In and out I went, my pace gradually increasing until I was taking her hard enough to drive the air from her lungs. Her breasts shook with each stroke, and it wasn't long before I gave into the temptation to lean down and take one plump nipple in my mouth.

Trisha whimpered as I scraped my teeth over the sensitive skin, and when her nails raked down my back, I hissed in pain. It mingled with the pleasure coiling inside me, pushing me closer to the edge. I rode that fine line as I drew more of her nipple into my mouth, worrying at it with my teeth even as I sucked on it. She writhed under me, as if she had too many sensations to process.

Then I heard it, the already-familiar hitch in her breathing.

"Close," she gasped, burying her fingers in my hair. "So close."

I raised my head, stretching her nipple until she cried out and then releasing it. "Then come for me, sweetheart."

I reached down and hooked my hand around the back of her knee, raising her leg to open her for me even more. When I drove in this time, I went deep, and she keened. I repeated the movement again and again, chanting her name until she finally stiffened, screaming out my name. I pumped into her two more times, her pussy impossibly tight, and then found my release.

As pleasure coursed through me, I collapsed on her, the two of us lost in ecstasy together. And somewhere in the back of my mind, I clung to that word.

Together.

# EPILOGUE

## *TRISHA*

A whirlwind, that's what the past month had been—a blur of cardboard boxes and bubble wrap, the musty scent of old books mixing with the crisp tang of new beginnings. Dad's laughter, warm and rich, cut through the bustle of moving day as Blaze hefted a box labeled 'Kitchen' into the apartment.

"Man, you sure know how to pack a punch with these boxes," Blaze said, muscles flexing under his shirt as he set the box down with a grunt. The simplicity of his gesture and the ease with which he had inserted himself into our lives were astonishing and heartwarming.

Dad clapped him on the back, a smile crinkling the corners of his bright blue eyes—eyes that mirrored

## M. S. PARKER

mine. "Couldn't have done it without you, son. You've been a rock for both of us." His voice, laced with gratitude, filled the small space, wrapping around us like a warm embrace.

The apartment was small but filled with light, every corner a promise of comfort. The windows offered views of Baltimore that I had already grown to love—its brick-laden streets and bustling neighborhoods were now part of my daily canvas.

Blaze caught my gaze and winked, his blue-violet eyes sparking with mischief. "I think he's settling in just fine."

As I looked around the apartment, watching Dad wander from room to room with a growing smile, I felt a wave of relief wash over me. This was right—this move, this city, this new chapter for all of us.

I stepped up to Dad, wrapping an arm around his shoulders. "You like it here?" I asked, even though his grin told me everything I needed to know.

"It's more than I imagined," Dad said, his voice steady and sure. "The doctors here are top-notch, Trisha. And having you—and Blaze—by my side? Well, I'm one lucky man."

My heart swelled at his words. The journey had been daunting: convincing him to leave San Francisco, finding the right place in Baltimore, ensuring he'd receive the care he needed. But here we were, standing in a testament to that effort.

Blaze slid an arm around my waist, pulling me close as we watched Dad explore his new home. "You did good," he whispered against my hair.

Turning to face him, I caught the pride in his expression—a reflection of my own feelings. "We did good," I corrected him softly.

Blaze had become more than just a partner in logistics; he'd become part of our family fabric—a thread woven in with care and steadfastness. His presence was a balm to the chaos that change often brought.

As we unpacked the last few boxes together, laughter and light conversation filling the space between us, I couldn't shake off the sense of contentment that settled deep within me. The upheaval that brought Blaze into my life—the canceled flights, the impromptu road trip—had led to something beautiful.

I paused amidst the clutter of half-unpacked belongings and let out a breath I didn't realize I'd been holding. Life was unpredictable; it could twist and turn in ways that left you dizzy. But sometimes, those detours led you exactly where you needed to be.

Dad popped open a bottle of sparkling cider, insisting on saving champagne for when all boxes were unpacked, and poured three glasses. We clinked them together in a makeshift toast.

"To new beginnings," Dad said with warmth.

"To family," Blaze added, squeezing my hand gently under the table.

I watched as Blaze navigated the cluttered space with an ease that spoke of a familiarity that had blossomed quickly over the past weeks. His flame-red wavy hair was a stark contrast to the neutral tones of the apartment walls, catching the fading light as the day gave way to evening.

"Hey, Trisha," Blaze called out, a certain lilt in his voice that snagged my attention. "What do you say we go out for dinner tonight? I've got something special I want to share with you."

A curious flutter danced in my stomach at his words. Dinner invitations weren't unusual between us, but there was an undercurrent of significance in his tone that wasn't there before. "Sure," I replied, trying to keep my voice even. "That sounds lovely."

Blaze flashed me a grin that reached all the way to his blue-violet eyes and left without another word, the promise of 'something special' hanging in the air like a secret waiting to be told.

As the door closed behind him, I found myself alone with a jumble of thoughts. My mind spun wildly with possibilities—could he be talking about a new job offer? A sudden insight into one of his many research projects? Or maybe something more personal?

I sank into one of the dining chairs we had just assembled, my fingers drumming against the wood. Blaze was not one for grand gestures or dramatic reveals; he was more of a steady presence, his actions always thoughtful and deliberate.

I pushed away from the table and wandered to the window, watching the Baltimore skyline transform under the dusky sky. The city was alive with possibilities, each light in the growing darkness a story unfolding. Just like ours.

With every minute that passed, my anticipation grew. I wasn't sure what Blaze had planned for this evening, but I knew it would be another stitch in our shared experiences—a moment that would linger long after dinner.

Dad's voice echoed from his room, snapping me out of my reverie. "You look miles away, kiddo," he said with a chuckle.

"Just thinking about Blaze's dinner invite," I confessed, turning away from the window.

"Well," Dad said as he joined me by the window, looking out at our new world, "Blaze hasn't steered us wrong yet."

"No," I agreed, a smile tugging at my lips. "He hasn't."

I glanced at my reflection in the glass—medium chestnut curls framing my face and electric blue eyes reflecting a mixture of nerves and excitement. Whatever Blaze had to tell me tonight, it was clear it would mark another turn in our ever-evolving journey—a journey I found myself more than ready to continue.

---

THE CHIME of the restaurant door signaled our entry into a world of culinary delights, the soft lighting and ambient music wrapping around us like a comforting embrace. Blaze's hand found the small of my back, guiding me to our table with an ease that spoke of our growing intimacy.

"I hope you're hungry," Blaze said with a playful glint in his eyes as we settled into our seats. "I've heard the chef here doesn't take kindly to uneaten plates."

I chuckled, scanning the menu. "Well, he hasn't met my appetite. It's practically legendary."

Our waiter arrived, and Blaze ordered for us both, a bold move that earned him an arched eyebrow from me. "Confident, aren't we?" I teased.

"Just wait, you'll be impressed," he assured me, his confidence infectious.

As the evening unfolded, our conversation meandered from lighthearted banter to deeper, more meaningful topics. We laughed over shared stories, our connection deepening with each shared anecdote and insight.

It was during dessert, as we indulged in a decadent chocolate creation, that Blaze's demeanor shifted to something more serious. He reached into his pocket, pulled out a small object, and slid it across the table toward me. It was a key.

"This," he began, his voice soft yet certain, "is my way of saying I'm ready for more. For us."

I picked up the key, the cool metal a tangible symbol of the step we were taking. "This is big, Blaze. Moving in together big," I said, a mix of excitement and nervousness in my voice.

He nodded, his eyes meeting mine. "I know. And I wouldn't offer it if I wasn't sure. About us."

The weight of the moment settled between us, a beautiful promise of what was to come. I leaned forward, my hand covering his. "Thank you, Blaze. For this, for helping with Dad... for everything."

As we finished our meal, the topic shifted to the future—to plans, dreams, and the life we were building. "So, Professor Gracen," I said with a smirk, "ready to tackle the academic world with me?"

"Only if you promise not to grade me too harshly," he quipped, earning a laugh.

"I make no promises," I replied, grinning.

As we left the restaurant, I threw in a playful

suggestion. "Let's go test this key. You know, for... quality assurance purposes."

Blaze's laughter echoed in the night air, a perfect end to a perfect evening. "Lead the way, Dr. Easton."

Hand in hand, we walked through the streets, our steps light and hearts full. The promise of what lay ahead was exhilarating, a shared adventure that we were both eager to embark on. Tonight was just the beginning, and as we approached his apartment, key in hand, I knew our story was just getting started.

# THE END

# THE SCOTTISH BILLIONAIRES READING ORDER

*Alec & Lumen:*
Prequel
1. Off Limits
2. Breaking Rules
3. Mending Fate

*Eoin & Aline:*
1. Strangers in Love
2. Dangers of Love

*Brody & Freedom:*
1. Single Malt
2. Perfect Blend

*Baylen & Harlee:*
Business or Pleasure

## THE SCOTTISH BILLIONAIRES READING ORDER

*Drake & Maggie:*
At First Sight

*Carson & Vix:*
*A Dress for Curves*

*Spencer & London*
*A Play for Love*

Printed in Great Britain
by Amazon